Eclipse

Eclipse

Andrea Cheng

Front Street
Asheville, North Carolina

ALSO BY ANDREA CHENG

Marika

Honeysuckle House

The Lace Dowry

Copyright © 2006 by Andrea Cheng
All rights reserved
Printed in China
Designed by Helen Robinson
First edition

Library of Congress Cataloging-in-Publication Data
Cheng, Andrea.
Eclipse / Andrea Cheng.—1st ed.
p. cm.
Summary: In Cincinnati, Ohio, in the summer of 1952,
eight-year-old Peti gives up his room to his Hungarian relatives,
including a twelve-year-old cousin who bullies him, and worries about
his grandfather who cannot escape from behind the Iron Curtain.
ISBN-13: 978-1-932425-21-5 (alk. paper)
[1. Immigrants—Ohio—Fiction. 2. Hungarian Americans—Fiction.
3. Family life—Ohio—Fiction. 4. Ohio—History—20th century—Fiction.
5. Hungary—History—1945–1989—Fiction.] I. Title.
PZ7.C41943Ecl 2006
[Fic]—dc22
2006000785

Front Street
An Imprint of Boyds Mills Press, Inc.
A Highlights Company

815 Church Street
Honesdale, Pennsylvania 18431

To my family

1

Visa Ready Arriving Monday Olga Jozsef Gabor. The telegram says that on yellow paper. You pay by the word. That's why they left out *is* and *on* and *love* and *and*.

"What's a visa?" I ask Mom.

"Permission."

"Permission for what?"

"To come to America."

"Did we have a visa?"

"Yes, we had one too when we came."

"What if you come without the visa?"

"Then they send you to jail."

I don't want my aunt and uncle and cousin to go to jail. I'm glad they waited for the visa, even though it took so many years.

I play with a small helicopter that makes sparks when you turn the propeller. "Where does their airplane go?" I ask.

"From Sydney to Cincinnati."

I'm good with maps and directions. Sometimes Mom asks me to come with her in the car so I can tell her which way to turn. "Does it stop in Hawaii?"

"It stops in lots of places."

"Like where?"

"When we came, we stopped in the Fiji Islands and Hawaii and Los Angeles."

I wish I could remember being on the airplane, but I was too little. "I want to fly on an airplane," I say.

"You did."

"But I can't remember it."

"Someday we'll take an airplane again, Peti. Now stop talking so much." Mom is busy hammering meat to make it thin and tender the way Papa likes it. If it's tough, he'll push his plate aside and eat only bread.

I have one more question. "What's he like?"

"Who?"

"Gabor."

"I saw him only when he was a baby. He's a big boy now, much older than you."

I know. He's twelve and I'm eight. My neighbor Steven is twelve too. Sometimes he holds the back of my bike when I pedal so I won't fall down. He likes this helicopter too. We take it into the garage and shut the door and watch the sparks fly around. But some big boys are mean, like the two on the corner. They shout when I ride by and make me lose my balance and zoom down the driveway into the garbage cans.

"Is he nice?"

"He's your cousin. He plays the violin."

"That's all?"

Mom nods.

2

Aunt Olga and Uncle Jozsef and Gabor will stay in my room. Mom stands on a chair and sweeps away the spiderwebs with a broom. Aunt Olga likes everything very clean, Mom says. I have to clear off my desk. Mom says to throw away my paper airplanes. Underneath I find my special pen that has water in the top and a small plane inside that moves when you tilt it. My grandpa Apaguy in Hungary sent it to me for my birthday. I'm the only one who calls him Apaguy. Mom calls him Apa, which means "father" in Hungarian. Everyone calls me *papaguy*, "parakeet," because I repeat what people say. Papaguy and Apaguy.

I put the pen into my pocket. Mom is sweeping the floor now, but I want her to read me a book, maybe the one I took out of the library about the boy who traveled back in time. I can read it myself, but I like it when we read books together.

"Can you read me a book?"

Mom turns on the vacuum cleaner.

I hold the book right in front of her and shout. "Can you read me this book?"

"Peti, I am busy now. Go find something to do."

Mom's mouth is in a thin straight line. She won't change her mind even if I keep asking.

I take my helicopter and go outside. Steven is in the

driveway with a magnifying glass. "What are you doing?"
I ask.

"Burning stuff."

"What stuff?"

Steven doesn't look up. He is holding the magnifying glass very still over a leaf.

"My aunt and uncle and cousin are coming from Australia," I say.

Steven is making smoke come out of the leaf.

"They went from Hungary to Australia just like us, and now they are following us to America because they finally got a visa."

Steven still doesn't say anything.

"My cousin is twelve like you."

The smoke is making me cough. I want Steven to stop.

"Want to play with the helicopter?" Now I see that he is burning an ant with the magnifying glass. "What are you doing?"

"You talk too much," Steven says.

I should tape my mouth shut. The ant is scurrying away but Steven is chasing it with the point of light. It shrivels and smokes. I look away so I don't have to think about the ant. I take my pen out of my pocket and tilt it so the airplane moves back and forth. Someday I'll take an airplane far away. I'll visit Apaguy in Hungary. He won't tell me I talk too much. He can't visit us because he doesn't have a visa, so I have never even met him. He writes me letters and I write him back. Sometimes he sends me small packages and I send him drawings and my school photos.

I wish it was Apaguy who got a visa instead of Uncle Jozsef and Aunt Olga and Gabor. But the government won't give Apaguy one because he lives behind the Iron Curtain. It's not really a curtain. Papa explained it to me. It's an imaginary curtain, and the people who live behind it can't get out because their government won't let them. Too bad Hungary is behind that curtain, and other countries too, like Russia and Romania. Papa says there are soldiers at the border with machine guns who shoot anyone who tries to leave. I wonder how they even know exactly where the border is. On a map there's a line, but there can't be a line on the ground unless there's a river, like the one between Ohio and Kentucky.

Apaguy's letters take three or four weeks to get to our house. When we finally get them, sometimes they are torn or crumpled. Mom thinks some of Apaguy's letters never even make it. Maybe they're sitting in a post office in Budapest or maybe they've been burned in an incinerator. I'm lucky my special airplane pen didn't get burned.

Steven snatches the pen out of my hand. "Cool. Where'd you get that?"

"My grandpa sent it to me from Hungary."

"From where?"

"Hungary. It's next to Austria and Romania in central Europe."

"Can I borrow it?" Steven smiles. "Want to play helicopter in the garage?" He puts the pen into his pocket. "Come on."

The sparks look like firecrackers all around. Like stars in a planetarium. I borrowed a book from the school library about planets, moons, and stars. I was sad when I had to return it because I liked having the planets book next to my bed. When I couldn't sleep, I would look at all the galaxies.

Steven turns the propeller fast and moves the helicopter around so the light makes a figure eight. I laugh. He pretends the plane is about to crash and then swoops back up into the sky. He makes it land on top of my head.

"Well, Peter, I have to go." He hands the helicopter to me.

"Where's my pen?"

"I'm just borrowing it."

He opens the door of the garage and runs out into the bright sunshine. My pen is in his pocket. Maybe I should run after him, but he is crossing the street to where the mean boys are.

I sit in the cool shade of the garage and make airplane noises. Aunt Olga and Uncle Jozsef and Gabor are in a plane right now. Maybe they are over Siberia. I'd like to take a plane to Siberia because I like snow. Mom said Gabor never saw snow in Australia. This winter I'll show him how to make snowballs. I'll show him the icicle I took off the roof and put into our freezer. He won't believe we have icicles like that in America.

3

The airport is crowded. I look at all the boys who are about twelve and wonder which one is my cousin. Finally Mom points and says, *"Ott vannak,"* there they are. Aunt Olga is in front. She has light brown eyes with lots of lines around them, like Papa's. She and Papa look like twins, but I know they're not because Papa is fifteen months older.

She hugs me so hard I lose my breath. "Petike, my Petike," she says. Tears roll down her cheeks. She wipes them with hands that look like Papa's too, only smaller. Gabor stands apart. His eyes dart around.

"This is Peter," Aunt Olga says to Gabor. She could say "Peti" because Gabor knows Hungarian, just like me. Gabor looks down. Mom and Papa hug him but he doesn't hug back.

Uncle Jozsef hands me a red box. "Open it," he says.

"Now?"

"Go ahead."

I open the lid and inside is a bright red boomerang.

"The boys in Australia throw these all the time. Gabor will teach you," Uncle Jozsef says.

Gabor has moved over to the other side of the conveyor belt.

"Thanks." I hug Uncle Jozsef. Lots of people hug at the airport. Uncle Jozsef smells like Old Spice. I like that smell. I like the red boomerang so much.

We take six suitcases off the conveyor belt. Papa and Uncle Jozsef argue about who will carry which suitcase. Papa wants to carry the heaviest one. They start pulling it back and forth and shouting in Hungarian. Everyone is looking at us. Finally Mom says they are making a spectacle. Uncle Jozsef gives up and Papa carries the heavy suitcase.

In the car, Gabor says my boomerang isn't real so it won't come back when I throw it. His English words sound funny.

"That's okay," I say. "I still like it."

He shrugs.

"Why won't it come back?" I ask.

"I told you. It's not a real boomerang."

"Is it fake?"

He doesn't answer so I ask him in Hungarian. "*Igazi*?"

Gabor shuts his eyes and puts his head back on the seat. Aunt Olga says he has jet lag. Australia is fourteen hours ahead of us. That means Gabor has to repeat fourteen hours of his life. And that makes you very tired.

4

Uncle Jozsef and Aunt Olga and Gabor put their suitcases in
my room. Mom makes a special bed for me in the corner of
her room. She folds a feather *paplan* quilt in half and covers
it with a sheet to make a mattress. Then she puts a sheet on
top and gives me one of her pillows. I lie down on my new
bed and put the boomerang next to me on the floor.

"Good night, Peti," Mom says.

"When are you going to bed?" I ask.

"Later."

"What time?"

"I don't know, Peti. Good night."

"Mom?" I don't know what I was planning to ask. Words
come out of my mouth by themselves. "Is the boomerang
real or fake?"

"I don't know."

"Gabor says it's fake."

Mom pats my head. The air is hot but Mom's fingers are
cool on my forehead. "It doesn't matter, Peti."

"How long will I get to sleep in your room?"

"We'll see."

I don't like it when Mom says "We'll see." I like to know
the plans. I want to sleep in Mom and Papa's room forever.
I don't like having my own room with cracks that look like
spiderwebs on the walls. Maybe Aunt Olga and Uncle Jozsef

and Gabor will stay forever. But if my legs get long like Gabor's, I won't fit on the *paplan*. I'll have to unfold it.

"Good night, Peti."

Mom goes out into the living room. I sit up and turn on the reading light. Too bad I don't have the planets book anymore. My teacher said the regular library probably has other books about the solar system.

Next to the reading light is a small frame with a picture of me when I was a baby. I'm at the swimming pool with my round belly sticking out over the top of my shorts. I'm smiling and water is dripping off my hair. On the other side of the lamp is a framed picture of Apaguy with his arm around Mom. She looks the same as now except that her cheeks are fatter. Her head is touching Apaguy's and they're laughing. Now Mom laughs only when I say things in Hungarian that are a little bit wrong and sound funny. Then she writes those funny things to Apaguy so he can laugh in Hungary. They're laughing about the same thing but not at the same time or in the same place. It's been seven years since Mom has seen her father and now he's stuck behind that Iron Curtain. Whenever it's my birthday, I blow out my candles and wish Apaguy could come so Mom would laugh like in the picture.

I turn off the light. There's a lot of noise coming from my old room, suitcases banging and things falling onto the floor. Aunt Olga says, "Shhhh, Peti is asleep." After that they whisper so I can't hear the words.

The *paplan* is harder than a bed. I feel my hipbone

against the floor. What if my airplane pen gets stuck in the washing machine at Steven's house? Maybe I can sneak into his house and find his jeans on the floor and get my pen back. But he's only borrowing it. That's what he said.

I'm glad I don't have to repeat fourteen hours of my life because I might have to repeat Steven chasing the ant and burning it. My stomach churns. I'm sure Steven will give my pen back tomorrow. He helps me ride my bike. He doesn't play with the mean boys very much. Tomorrow I'll say, "Steven, I want my pen back," and he'll say, "Sure, here you go," and he'll toss it to me.

The door opens quietly. Mom comes in and goes to the closet to get her nightgown. She stops, and even with my eyes closed I know she is looking at me. I don't move. She wants me to be asleep. Her footsteps go over to her side of the bed. I hear the sound of her glasses on the nightstand and the covers shuffling and the bed creaking. I know she is waiting for Papa to come up but he is still watching the news on television. He never comes up until he has watched the news because something very important might have happened during the day. Like now there's a war in Korea, and even though we don't have any relatives there, Papa wants to know because everything is related to everything else. I know that's true because even the Earth is connected to all the other planets and the whole solar system. Papa wants us to be ready in case something bad happens like another war with the Nazis. The Nazis almost killed Mom and Papa, but they don't like to talk about that anymore.

The thing is, I don't know how you're supposed to get ready for things if you don't know what they are. Papa has the volume on the television turned up very loud because he doesn't want to miss a single word.

5

Uncle Jozsef and Gabor are shouting because Gabor doesn't want to practice his violin. They start in Hungarian and switch to English. Gabor calls his father bad names. He is lying on my old bed and tossing a pair of socks up to the ceiling over and over. I watch through the crack in the door. Uncle Jozsef says, "You will never amount to anything." Gabor keeps on tossing the socks. Aunt Olga says, "You'd better listen to your father." Then Uncle Jozsef grabs the socks and Gabor says, "Hey, those are mine. Give them back."

"Peti." Mom pulls me away from the door. "What are you doing?"

"I want to go in and get my book."

"You can wait until later."

I follow Mom to the kitchen. "Gabor is not nice," I say.

"He needs time to adjust," Mom says. "It's all different in Australia."

"How long will it take?"

Mom sighs. "I don't know."

"How is it different?"

Mom is stirring Cream of Wheat on the stove. I like the way the bubbles grow and pop. She puts some into a bowl for me and I feel the warm sweetness on my tongue.

Now Gabor is practicing his scales. Then he plays a really fast song.

Aunt Olga and Uncle Jozsef come into the kitchen for breakfast. "Gabor will be here after he finishes practicing," Uncle Jozsef says.

I hope Mrs. Wilson who lives downstairs likes the violin. There are lots of things she doesn't like. Seeing my bicycle in the hallway is one.

After breakfast I go outside and knock on Steven's door. His brother says he's not home, so I sit on the sidewalk and wait. There are lots of tiny ants. I make them a farm with a tiny fence out of twigs and a grass barn. They like their new home in the dirt. They don't have to worry about a beam of hot light. I make a small hill and put a tree on top. That would be a good place for a tire swing. Steven is still not home.

I go and get my boomerang. It's so shiny and clean. I take it out and stand by the curb. I wonder how you're supposed to throw it. I could wait for Gabor to be done practicing, but I'm tired of waiting. I throw it hard like a baseball into the air.

It lands in the middle of the street. A car could come and crush it. I run out fast and pick it up and dust it off. It's just a little dirty, that's all. No, now I see that there's a small crack on the left side. But a small crack won't hurt a boomerang.

Mom grabs my arm. "Peti, you are going to kill yourself standing in the middle of the street." She is about to spank me but she doesn't. Instead she hugs me. "Petike, you have to be more careful."

I run upstairs and put the boomerang back under my *paplan*. Then I lie down and cry without noise so nobody will know. I want my pen back and I want the boomerang not to have a crack. Gabor plays his song perfectly. The notes are clear and strong. I hear the violin case shut and then it is quiet.

Later, when I look out the window, Gabor and Steven are standing with the two mean boys on the corner, looking up at our house and laughing. I duck down under the windowsill so they can't see me. I should have stayed outside and waited for Steven. Then I would have my pen back and he wouldn't be playing with my cousin and those mean boys. He'd be with me in the garage instead.

I hear the laughing again, but I don't look out this time.

6

Uncle Jozsef looks at the newspaper and circles the jobs that maybe he can get. Mom says he should take his time, rest up a little, but he says there's no time to rest when you have a wife and a son and no job. He circles *Accountant*, *Bookkeeper*, and *Mechanic*.

"You are certainly not a mechanic," Aunt Olga says. "You couldn't even fix the sewing machine."

"Nobody could fix that sewing machine."

"The mechanic fixed it, remember?"

"He was not a mechanic. He was a sewing-machine repairman."

Uncle Jozsef takes out the bag of shoe polish and rags, and I polish his shoes. I smear the black paste in circles. When it's dry, we start buffing. I do it so fast that soon the shoes shine like a mirror.

"Watch out, you'll wear down the leather," Uncle Jozsef warns, but he's kidding. He says his shoes have never looked so good, almost brand-new. With shoes like that, he's sure to find a job. I get some polish on my shirt and a little on the floor.

Uncle Jozsef wears a suit even though it's hot outside. The suit makes him look more professional. After he leaves, Aunt Olga and Mom talk about the job Uncle Jozsef might have when he gets home.

"Accountant would be a good job," Aunt Olga says. "Jozsef is good with figures."

Mom nods.

"Jozsef is a very organized man. That's good for book-keeping, you know."

"Yes," Mom says.

Aunt Olga is ironing and Mom is darning socks. Gabor must still be asleep. "Can I play with the darning egg?" I ask.

"I'm using it now, Peti," Mom says.

When I was in kindergarten, I got sick, and Mom made the darning egg into a puppet named Maxi. She had a doll named Maxi when she was little. During the war, she thought she had lost him because her house got hit by a bomb. But later, when she went back to see what was left in the rubble, the housekeeper came out of the basement with a paper bag, and Maxi was inside it. Mom had to leave poor Maxi behind when she went to America. She couldn't carry very many things. I wish she had put Maxi in her bag. He wasn't heavy but she had other things to think about, she says.

To make my Maxi, Mom drew two round eyes and eyebrows and a small nose on the darning egg with a black pen. She used a red pen for the round mouth. Now my Maxi is covered by one of Papa's brown socks, and Mom is weaving new thread into the heel.

I smell something burning. Mom jumps up but it's too late. The beans boiled over on the stove and burned. Aunt Olga says we can still eat them. They're not that burned. She and Mom try to separate the very burned part from the not-so-burned part, and then they scrub the stove with steel wool.

The mailman comes with a blue envelope, but it's from Mom's brother in Budapest, not from Apaguy. Mom stops darning and looks at the return address.

"Usually it's my father who writes," she tells Aunt Olga.

"This time your brother decided to write."

Mom's face is white. "Something must have happened." She's always worried about Apaguy living behind that Iron Curtain.

"Not necessarily," Aunt Olga says.

"Open it," I say.

Mom slits the envelope carefully along the edge, then pulls out the thin paper and unfolds it. Her eyes move quickly over the words.

"They took Apa," she says.

"Took him where?" Aunt Olga asks.

"To a farm in Tapioszele."

"Who took him?" I ask. Nobody is listening to me. "Apaguy will like the farm," I say, louder.

"Be quiet, Peti."

"Read it out loud," Aunt Olga says.

The letter is short. Mom mumbles the Hungarian words:

Dear Marika,
    Apa is on a farm in Tapioszele. We don't know when

he'll be coming home. In the meantime, he will be helping
the farmer. I'll visit him there and write you when I get
home. I hope you and the family are doing well.

  With much love,

  Andras

  PS Mail letters to me and I will deliver them.

   I wish I lived on a real farm like Apaguy so I could have a cat. Mom says a cat would be too much trouble. What I really want is a small kitten. I bet Apaguy has lots of cats and maybe even some kittens on the farm.

   Mom puts her head down on the table. I think she's crying. Aunt Olga is patting her back. Aunt Olga is not Mom's sister, but she seems like it.

   "It's okay," Aunt Olga says. "It's for only a short time."

   "He survived the war. And now this?"

   Aunt Olga is still patting. "You'll see. It won't be so bad."

   "That's what we said before."

   Aunt Olga cuts Mom off. "Shhh, Marika, you'll see."

   Mom gets up and washes her face at the kitchen sink.

   "I want to live on a farm too," I say. "It would be fun to have a cat."

   Nobody listens to my words. I don't know why Mom is crying. Living on a farm is not so terrible. Maybe Apaguy likes it there.

   "What if from the farm they take him someplace far away?" Mom asks.

"They won't do that," Aunt Olga says. "Your brother said Tapioszele. That's only about sixty kilometers from Budapest. Maybe not even that far."

I get the atlas and look up Hungary. I try to find Tapioszele but it's not marked. There's a tiny dot that could be it. I show Mom the dot but she barely glances at it.

"He could be taken to Siberia next, for all I know," she says.

"I wish I could see Siberia," I say.

"He might be starving," Mom says.

Aunt Olga shakes her head. "Nobody starves on a farm."

"How about in winter?"

"He'll be home long before winter," Aunt Olga says.

Mom takes the letter back out of the envelope and rereads it. "I can't understand my brother. He says Apa is on a farm. But he doesn't say how he got there. My father is a sixty-year-old stockbroker. What on earth can he do to help a farmer?"

"The letters are censored," Aunt Olga says. "We have to read between the lines."

"So what does it really mean?" Mom asks.

Aunt Olga takes the letter and rereads it herself.

"What does 'censored' mean?" I ask.

"It means that somebody reads the letters," Aunt Olga says.

"We'd better see if Mr. Kadar can do something," Mom says.

Papa already told us about Mr. Kadar, who works with him at the hospital. Mom tells Aunt Olga that Mr. Kadar has a sister in Hungary who can maybe help because she has friends in the government. "He offered to ask her once before," Mom adds.

"Good. You'll see, Apa will not stay on the farm for long."

Mom goes to the telephone to call Papa. She tells him about the letter from her brother. While she talks, her voice keeps cracking. She asks him to invite Mr. Kadar to our apartment as soon as possible. Gabor comes out of his room finally and sits at the kitchen table, but whatever Aunt Olga offers to fix him for breakfast he doesn't want.

The doorbell rings. It is Mrs. Wilson, in her bathrobe. "There is a lot of noise up here," she says, looking around.

"I'm sorry," Mom says. "We'll try to be more quiet. You know how boys are."

"You can have only three people in this apartment." Mrs. Wilson stares at Aunt Olga.

"This is my husband's sister," Mom says. "And my nephew. They are visiting from Australia."

"I see." Mrs. Wilson turns to head down the stairs. I wait for her to say something about my bicycle but she doesn't.

When she disappears, I ask, "Why does Mrs. Wilson care how many people are in the apartment?"

"Mrs. Wilson is nosy. That's why. And she is the landlady."

After that Mom washes the kitchen floor with a brush.

Aunt Olga says to relax but Mom won't stop scrubbing. A small piece of linoleum breaks off. Mom sticks it back where it was.

I go outside and knock on Steven's door again. This time his mother answers. She calls for Steven and he comes down the stairs, but when he sees me, he stops.

"Hey, Peter, what's up?"

"I need my pen."

"What pen? You want to borrow a pen? Here." He tosses me a black pen. I want to throw it back and say, "No, my airplane pen," but Steven's mom is right there. Then Steven says he has to go and they close the door. I throw the black pen onto the sidewalk and step on it.

When I go back inside, Mom is waxing the floor. "I'm good at buffing," I tell her. "I practiced on Uncle Jozsef's shoes."

Mom smiles a little and gives me a flannel rag. I make big, fast circles on the floor until it shines. I can see my reflection in the shiny floor. It shows bumps in my face wherever there are bumps in the linoleum. When my arm gets tired, I switch to my left hand.

"Why did Apaguy have to move to the farm if he didn't want to?" I ask.

Mom is filling the bucket with soapy water. "The government forced him."

"Does the government force everyone?"

"Not everyone. Only people they don't like."

"Why don't they like Apaguy?"

"Because he was a stockbroker, and they don't like stockbrokers."

"Why not?"

Mom is scrubbing the cabinet doors. Water drips onto the floor that I waxed and forms little beads. "It's too complicated, Peti," Mom says. She dumps the dirty water into the sink and squeezes out the sponge.

I keep on buffing. I'll make the floor so shiny that Mrs. Wilson will not care how many people we have in our apartment. When I grow up, maybe I'll clean houses. I like it when everything sparkles. Or maybe I'll be a mailman. I'll definitely never be a stockbroker.

7

Gabor doesn't look up when I come in. He's reading the comics. I don't like comics much. Usually they're not funny until Papa explains them to me, and Papa's at work. Mom is writing a letter.

"Why don't you two boys play outside," Aunt Olga says.

Gabor acts like he doesn't hear anything. He has on shorts, and his long legs are sticking way out from under the table. His legs are covered with hair. I know he doesn't want to play with me. "Is Steven out?" he asks me.

"He's in his house and he won't give me my pen back." Gabor shrugs.

"But it's a special pen that I got from Apaguy."

Mom looks up. "The one with the airplane?"

I nod.

"Why did you give it to him?"

"I didn't. He took it."

"You shouldn't have taken it outside," Mom says. "A pen belongs in the house."

"Gabor will get it back for you," Aunt Olga says.

I go outside and get on my bike and ride really, really fast up and down the street because now I am good at riding. I go around the small block and the big block a bunch of times. I'll get my pen back somehow. I'll creep into Steven's house at night and get it back.

Gabor is outside when I get home. "Want me to get your pen back?" he asks in a whisper.

I wait.

"Do you?"

I nod.

"Then you have to go upstairs to your old room, and in the biggest suitcase on the floor there's a pocket on the right side with money in it. Go get twenty dollars and bring it down to me and I'll get your pen back."

What if I get the dollars but Gabor doesn't get my pen? What if Steven put the pen somewhere?

Aunt Olga and Mom are in the kitchen talking softly. I go to my room. The black suitcase. The right pocket. There are no singles, only ten-dollar bills. I think Gabor wanted one-dollar bills, twenty of them.

I go back out and tell Gabor, "There were only ten-dollar bills."

"So? Get two."

"Two ten-dollar bills?"

"Why do you always repeat everything? You *are* a *papaguy.* Yes. Two tens."

I run up, get the money, and give it to him.

"Okay. Now go into the garage and wait."

"The garage? For how long?"

"Count to one hundred."

"Fast or slow?"

"Slow."

When I'm on seventy-six, he comes back with my

airplane pen. "Where did you get my pen?" I ask.

"Do you want it or not?"

"Yes, I want it."

He tosses it to me. I take the pen upstairs, sit on my *paplan,* and write a letter to Apaguy. When I write in Hungarian, I have to sound the words out carefully. I tell Apaguy that my neighbor took my airplane pen but I got it back. I don't write anything about the ten-dollar bills. Then I tell him that I hope he likes it on the farm, but if he doesn't, he should just go back to his old apartment. It's not fair for people to make other people do things they don't want to do. I tell him that Mom was crying about the farm.

When I give Mom the letter, she says she can't send it. "Because they read the letters, Peti. This can get Apaguy in trouble."

"In trouble. How?"

"We have to write letters very carefully so that Apaguy knows what we mean but nobody else knows." Mom hands the letter back to me.

"So I can't send it?"

"No."

"I got my pen back."

"I know. You wrote."

I don't know how I can write a letter to Apaguy that only he can understand. I ride my bike to the library because it has air conditioning and I'm tired of Mom's red eyes and Gabor's hairy legs and Aunt Olga begging Gabor to eat a little something.

At the library I ask Mrs. Malone how you can write letters that say one thing but mean something else, and she gives me three books about secret codes. I finish two of them before I leave.

8

Uncle Jozsef comes home every day for two weeks with nothing but the paper. He says that lots of the jobs we see in the ads aren't real.

"How can there be fake jobs?" I ask.

"They always say, 'I'm sorry, sir, the position has already been filled.'"

I look down at Uncle Jozsef's shoes. They are scratched and dull already. "I can polish your shoes," I say.

He takes them off and hands them to me, and I swirl the polish smoothly all around the toe and the sides and the back of each one. I buff them until they look new. Uncle Jozsef does the crossword puzzle and listens to records. "Someday Gabor will play like that," he says.

Gabor wants to toss a baseball with me. First it's fun. He throws the balls up high so I have time to get ready. Sometimes I miss but sometimes the ball lands in my mitt. Then he starts throwing the ball too hard.

"That hurts," I say.

"Do you want to learn how to play baseball or not?"

I don't answer.

"I can't just throw baby balls all the time."

He sends a line drive. I put my mitt up and the ball hits so hard that it stings through all the padding. When I take off the mitt, my whole hand is red and throbbing. Gabor tosses his glove on the ground and goes to find Steven. I start to follow but he tells me to find somebody my own age to play with.

But who? There's nobody my age on our street. In September when I go to third grade there will be thirty kids my age in my class, but in second grade they all said I talked too much. And they said I talked funny. Mom and Papa have a Hungarian accent, so I have one too, a little. Papa says if the other kids could speak two languages as well as I do, they would be happy, but they don't know anything about languages. At school I looked out the window a lot. There was a small yellow bird making a nest on the window ledge, so I watched that instead of listening to Mrs. Goodman. Then when we had a test, I couldn't finish even half of the questions. Mom asked if I could stay in second grade, but Mrs. Goodman said that would hurt my feelings.

I go inside. Mom and Aunt Olga aren't home. They probably went to practice driving because soon Aunt Olga is going to take the test for her driver's license. Next to the rocking chair in Mom's sewing basket is my Maxi. His face has faded but I can still see the dark eyes and the half smile.

I go behind the couch with Maxi. He says that is a safe place to be. We move up and down along the windowsill, but when we see Gabor or Steven or one of the other boys, we duck.

"Peti, why don't you play outside with the boys?"

Mom asks as soon as she comes home. "It's too dusty back there."

Aunt Olga pulls me to her lap. "Sit here with me, Petike. And who is this? Your little friend?"

"Maxi."

"You baby him," Mom says to Aunt Olga.

My aunt puts her cheek to my hair. "That's okay. Believe me, they grow up fast enough." She sees Gabor outside with the boys. "I'm glad Gabor has made some friends."

Mom nods. "Steven is a good boy."

"Not anymore," I say.

"Shhh, Peti, they are just bigger than you," Mom says.

I almost say something about the two ten-dollar bills, but what if Gabor finds out that I told? My hands are still raw from the baseball.

Outside, the boys are taking turns riding a fancy red bike with silver stripes on the frame. I've never seen that bike before. It looks brand-new.

"I guess Steven has a new bike," Mom says, glancing out the window.

I want to try that bike but I know I won't be able to reach the pedals. Anyway, the other kids would never let me have a turn. Now they are arguing. I go down to the front porch to listen. Steven says the bike should stay in his garage because it's mostly his. One of the other boys says it's not. They split the cost four ways. Gabor says that without his twenty dollars they would never have had enough. His twenty dollars. The blood rushes to my face. Steven says one bike is not enough for four people. They have to get another one. After that they huddle together and I can't hear what they're saying.

I go back in and lie down on my *paplan* with the helicopter and feel the boomerang under my pillow. Now it's all scratched up. Shoe polish might help hide the scratches.

I go back to the kitchen, take out the bag with the polish, and try to match the color. We don't have red polish but there is a sort of reddish brown. I swirl it all over the plastic and buff it with the cloth. The polish doesn't stick. It gets all over the linoleum.

"Peti, stop it," Mom says. "Mrs. Wilson will be unhappy if we ruin the linoleum."

"Mrs. Wilson is mean," I say.

Uncle Jozsef comes in with no job. Aunt Olga and Mom set the table for dinner. It's one of the tough-meat days. Papa takes only one bite of the stew. Mom's mouth is in the thin straight line. I know she hammered the meat, but it's still hard to chew. That's because it's the cheap meat, the part the butcher almost threw away.

"Have you talked to Mr. Kadar yet?" Mom asks.

"He was too busy today."

"Tell him it's important."

"Leave it to me, will you?" Papa says.

Uncle Jozsef and I eat lots of stew. It will make Mom happy if we eat her dinner. Gabor has only a little bit. He wants to go back outside, but Uncle Jozsef says he has to practice the violin. Gabor says he won't. They start shouting and Gabor calls his father bad names again. They go into my old room and shut the door but I can still hear all the shouting and banging around.

I go outside. Steven lets me look at the big red bike as long as I don't touch it.

"Hey, your cousin said you got a boomerang," he says.

"Yup."

"A real one?"

"Yup."

"Can I see it?"

Should I take it out? Mom said a pen was not for the outdoors but a boomerang is. The Aborigines threw boomerangs across the desert. I run upstairs to get it.

Steven holds it with both hands. "Have you tried to throw it?"

"Yup. But it didn't come back."

Steven throws it up in the air. It hovers for a minute and lands on the grass. We keep trying. Sometimes it comes back a little. Steven says you have to flick your wrist.

"Hey, can I borrow your boomerang?" Steven asks.

"No." I say it loud.

"Hey, sorry about the pen. But you got it back."

"I know."

"So why can't I borrow the boomerang?"

"You can't."

"Just for one day. I want to show it to my cousin. Look, you want to take a ride on the red bike with me?"

The bike is gleaming in the setting sun. I sit on the seat

and dangle my legs. Steven stands on the pedals, and we fly around the block, twice, three times.

"You want to go again?" Steven asks.

"Yup."

This time we go down past the grocery store and the Dairy Queen. Everybody waiting in line to buy ice cream can see me with my big friend on the red bike.

When we get back to my porch, Steven picks up the boomerang and winks at me. "Until tomorrow," he says.

9

Steven is gone for the rest of the week. Gabor says he went to visit his cousin in Indiana. Steven didn't tell me that his cousin lived far away.

Gabor says he knows where the boomerang is. "Go get me two more ten-dollar bills and I'll get it back for you," Gabor says.

"No," I say.

"Then no boomerang. And no more bicycle rides."

Gabor turns away from me. I go look for Maxi, but he's not in the sewing basket. I still have my helicopter, so I go in the garage and shut the door and watch the sparks fly. But I can't make as many sparks as Steven does. I sit in the cool darkness until my eyes adjust. Now I can see tiny ants crawling on the concrete.

The door opens and there is Gabor. "Want a ride on the red bicycle?"

I don't answer. The sunlight is blinding me.

"Get the money and I'll give you a ride." Gabor comes into the garage and shuts the door again. "I'll tell you a secret. If you get the money, we'll get another bicycle and you can ride it whenever you want."

"It's too big for me."

"We'll get a smaller one."

"Just like the other one, only smaller?"

My eyes are used to the dark and I can see Gabor's face. It looks nice when he smiles. "Yup. And guess what else? I'll get your boomerang back."

My room smells like Old Spice and shaving cream. I already know which pocket has the money. There are all the dollars. This time I'll take only one ten-dollar bill. One is not that many.

I run to the garage, but Gabor isn't there yet. I can take the money back to the suitcase. Nobody will know. I can tell Gabor that he can get the money himself. Where is he, anyway? Can it take so long to get my boomerang?

A shadow falls over me. "Here," Gabor says, handing me the boomerang.

I don't reach for it at first.

"Don't you even want it anymore?"

"It doesn't come back."

"Yes, it does. You just don't know how to throw it."

"You said it was fake."

"I was just kidding."

He takes the ten-dollar bill out of my fingers. Now he has the money and the boomerang. He's holding the boomerang above his shoulder as if he's going to throw it over the garage roof to the street behind us. I might never find it down there. It might crack into a million pieces. I jump and snatch the boomerang out of his hand.

10

Steven gets home in the afternoon. He and Gabor go into the woods behind the house, and soon I smell smoke. They motion for me to join them. Steven is holding his magnifying glass, and they are making a small campfire out of dry leaves. I won't go. I'll hide with Maxi behind the couch.

Mom and Aunt Olga aren't home. They went to the grocery-store parking lot to practice driving again. Aunt Olga is scared she's going to have an accident. She says people drive all over the road and you never know what they're going to do. Really she's the one who is all over the road. She says she's confused because in Australia they drive on the other side of the street, but she drives on the sidewalk and I don't think they do that anywhere. I think I could drive better than Aunt Olga.

I grab Maxi out of the sewing basket and lie on my back on the carpet. Now I can talk to Maxi as loud as I want. I tell him I hate all those big boys and I wish Gabor never got a visa. "I hate Gabor, I hate Gabor," I chant. "I want Gabor to fly to Siberia." I move Maxi in the air like he's an airplane.

Somebody has hold of my legs. I drop Maxi.

"Here's how it feels to fly on a plane." Gabor's voice is deep and quiet. He's pulling me by my legs around the bedrooms and the living room and the kitchen and back to the living room. I don't know where I am anymore. There are cracks in the walls, big cracks and smaller cracks and spiderwebs and cold linoleum with cracks and a tan fuzzy carpet.

I hold my head up so it won't bump but my shirt is up under my armpits and the rug is burning my skin. "Stop, stop," I beg.

"Tell me again what you said."

"Stop, please, stop."

"Before that."

I'll tape my mouth shut so I won't talk too much. Not even to Maxi. That's the problem. I talk too much.

We're going around Mom and Papa's room. I hit my arm on the leg of the bed. Gabor is slowing down. He's getting tired. The front door opens. The room is spinning so much that all I see are the cracks in the ceiling like a spiderweb. My old room has those big cracks but it smells like Uncle Jozsef and Old Spice now. My back hurts so I roll over as best I can. Gabor gasps.

"Just stay here," he says. There's fire in my skin, hot like the flames of the campfire, like the smoking ant.

Gabor comes back with ice in a dishtowel. The cold feels good on my skin but there isn't enough ice for it to be everywhere at once. I cry. Gabor shuts the door.

"Shhh. Sorry. Shhh."

I keep crying. The ice is turning to water all around me. Gabor gets a towel and I lie on that. "Ice all over," I whisper. He gets more ice from the freezer and spreads it out on my back.

"Sorry. I didn't mean to." His voice is choked.

I open my eyes but all I can see are his hairy legs. Then I see a big long icicle. "Put it back," I whisper.

"What?"

"Put it back."

"This?" He holds up the icicle.

I nod.

"Okay. I'll put it right back. You won't tell, will you?"

I take an ice cube and put it on my eyelids.

"Hey, Peti, you won't tell, right? Here, I'll get you another towel to dry off and a clean shirt. There. Now nobody will know, right, Peti?"

My eyes are shut to keep out the fire.

"Peter?"

More ice, and more and more and more. But not my icicle.

"Peti, when we get the new bike, you can ride it whenever you want, okay?"

I don't care about riding a bike except that the wind would be so cool and dry on my skin.

11

Mom comes in to say good night. My skin hurts so much I can hardly move. Mom says, "Are you okay, Peti? You were so quiet at dinner."

"Yes."

She pats my head. "You'll get your room back when Uncle Jozsef finds a job. Then he and Aunt Olga and Gabor will get their own apartment."

"I like this *paplan* bed," I whisper. "But I don't like Gabor."

"He needs time to get adjusted," Mom says.

I almost tell her. I almost do. But Mom cried again this morning about Apa on the farm. She sends letters to her brother, but we haven't gotten one from him or Apa in a long time. Mom told Aunt Olga that her father must have been taken somewhere else. Maybe they put him in prison or maybe he's not even alive anymore. Aunt Olga said, "Shhh, they aren't killing anyone. They're not going to put someone in prison who was not involved in politics." Then Mom reminded Aunt Olga that Apaguy was a stockbroker. Aunt Olga didn't say anything after that.

At dinner Gabor was nice. He gave me the crispy part of the chicken that he knows I like best. If I tell Mom, he'll throw the baseball so hard he'll break my hand. Aunt Olga will cry. She cried this morning because Gabor called her a bad name and he wouldn't practice and Uncle Jozsef hasn't found a job. Mom and Aunt Olga cry, and I do too, but Gabor and Papa and Uncle Jozsef don't. Or maybe they do, but they wait until nobody's watching. Sometimes when I feel like crying, I try not to, but it doesn't work.

Mom turns off the light. "Sleep well, Peti," she says.

It's impossible to sleep with your back on fire. I get up and put a cool washcloth on my skin. There's a fan in the window, and I stand with my pajama shirt up and the wind cooling off my back. Then I lie down again and think about the Earth and the stars and the sun and time around the world. It's ten o'clock in Cincinnati, so it's four in the morning in Hungary and noon in Australia and three in the afternoon in Siberia. I want to go someplace cold like that to cool off my skin.

In the morning I try to look at my back in the mirror, but when I twist, my skin hurts so much that my eyes tear up. I can see red streaks on my shoulders and the edges of the streaks are starting to scab. I put on a T-shirt and go to the kitchen for breakfast.

Papa is just about ready to leave for work. "Remember, Mr. Kadar is coming over for dinner tonight," he says to Mom.

"Yes, I remember," Mom says. Finally Mr. Kadar will come and help. Mom tells Aunt Olga that they will go to the meat market and buy the good beef today.

"But it's so expensive," Aunt Olga says.

"For Mr. Kadar, we have to," Mom says. "We'll make goulash to remind him of home."

"You're right," Aunt Olga says. "And I'll make a meat loaf with hard-boiled eggs and sausage inside and cucumber salad and *palacsinta*."

"Can I help?" I ask.

Aunt Olga tousles my hair. "Yes, Peti, you can be the chef's assistant."

Even though I'm too big, I sit on Aunt Olga's lap while she finishes her toast. Mom is busy making a shopping list.

"Do you want to come with us to the store?" Mom asks.

"Is Aunt Olga driving?" I ask.

Mom nods. "She has to practice."

"I'll stay home," I say.

Mom and Aunt Olga leave to get the ingredients for our dinner. I sit at Mom's desk and write a letter to Apaguy. It takes me longer than usual to sound out the Hungarian words.

Dear Apaguy,

Mr. Kadar is coming today!!! We are making beef stew with carrots and meat loaf and cucumber salad and palacsinta, my favorite dessert. Mr. Kadar is very important because his sister has a friend in the government who will help you go back home and then soon you can come to America. What I want to know is if you have a cat on the farm or not. I always want to get a kitten, but Mom says she has enough to take care of. Please write her to let me get a kitten because I'll take care of it myself.

    Love, your grandson,

    Peti

Then I remember that Mom said I should write something that only Apaguy will understand and nobody else. I erase the part about Mr. Kadar's friend and write, "Mr. Kadar is a very helpful person who will help you travel." That's better. "Travel" could mean anything. The rest of the letter will be okay.

I draw a small picture of an airplane on the bottom of the paper. Then I put the letter in an envelope and get a stamp out of the top desk drawer and copy my uncle's address from one of his old letters. The name of the street is long. There are eleven letters in it. I write *Air Mail* on the front and the back of the envelope even though it's an air-mail envelope, just to make sure they don't put my letter on a boat. Then I walk down to the mailbox and drop the letter in.

12

The batter is too thin and the *palacsinta* tears into pieces when Mom tries to flip it.

"Add more flour," Aunt Olga says.

Mom does, but then the batter is lumpy and the *palacsinta* is too thick. "I can't do it," Mom says. "I'm wasting the ingredients."

"No you aren't, because I'm eating the messed-up *palacsintas*," I say. I don't care if they're torn or whole. They taste just fine.

Mom sits down at the kitchen table and puts her head in her hands.

Aunt Olga is bustling around the kitchen, finishing up her meat loaf. I smell something burning. Aunt Olga runs to take the skillet off the burner. I open the kitchen door as wide as it goes because Papa hates the smell of burned things. It smells like we burned the house down.

"Don't worry. The rest will be fine," Aunt Olga says. She throws the burned *palacsinta* into the garbage can. Then she adds an egg to the *palacsinta* batter, cleans the burned skillet, and starts over. Her *palacsinta* is round and thin and perfect.

I help Aunt Olga make the rest of the dinner. I peel and slice the cucumbers for the cucumber salad. I cut the carrots for the goulash. We set the table with a tablecloth that has a stain on one side. Nobody will notice the stain because I put a ceramic tile on top of it. Mom keeps saying, "Thank you, thank you," to Aunt Olga, and "What would I do without you?" Then she says, "What if Mr. Kadar can't do anything to help Apa?"

"Wait and see," Aunt Olga says.

"I wrote Apaguy a letter today," I say, but they aren't listening to me.

"Why hasn't my brother written in so long?" Mom asks.

"The mail is unreliable," Aunt Olga says. "The letters could be sitting somewhere."

Mr. Kadar is so wrinkly. He shakes everyone's hand, even mine. "You must be Peter," he says to me in English. "I have heard so much about you from your father."

"You have?" After I say it, I think it was the wrong thing to say. But I really am surprised.

Mr. Kadar has moved on to Gabor. Gabor barely shakes his hand. He goes back into his room and won't come out for dinner even though Aunt Olga begs him. I wish she wouldn't do that. The begging never works. Then Aunt Olga says that Gabor isn't feeling well, which is a lie.

Mom is dressed in a pretty silk dress that rustles when she sits down, and I smell the perfume Apa gave her in a tiny bottle when she left Hungary. She had room in her bag to take the perfume but not enough room for Maxi. She uses only a very tiny bit every once in a while.

Mom puts lots of food on everyone's plate. Mr. Kadar

says he hasn't had a real Hungarian meal in a long time. He eats all his goulash and asks for more. I eat mine too. The grownups talk about the weather and how hot it is in Cincinnati. Then Mr. Kadar says he went to Sydney once and what a nice city it is, but Mom and Papa and Aunt Olga and Uncle Jozsef don't say anything. They hate Sydney. Everyone does, except Gabor.

"Sydney is very unfriendly," I say.

"Is that so?" Mr. Kadar smiles at me but Mom looks irritated that I said that.

Then Papa says that he and Mom are very worried about Mom's father. They haven't heard from him in several weeks. They know he was sent to a farm in Tapioszele, but they are not even sure if he is still there.

Mr. Kadar looks around the table. His eyes settle on me. "Maybe you should go play, Peter," he says. "Here, I have something for you." He reaches into his pocket and motions for me to come closer. He hands me a box with small beans in it. "Do you know what these are?"

"Beans."

"What kind of beans?" he asks.

"What kind of beans? I'm not sure," I say.

"Mexican jumping beans. Put them under a warm light and they'll move."

"Really?"

"Go try it."

"*Koszonom*," I tell him. He smiles because I thanked him in Hungarian.

I go into Mom and Papa's room and hold the beans under the lamp next to the photos. Nothing happens. I decide to leave them there for a few minutes. I go to the doorway and peek around the edge of the door so I can see the grownups.

Mr. Kadar is the only one talking. His voice is deep and the Hungarian words pour quickly out of his mouth. First he says that there is a shortage of things like matches and coffee in Hungary, so maybe we should send a package to Mom's brother, but make it small, less than a kilo, or it will never get there. Better yet, make the small package into several smaller ones. Then he takes a deep breath and says that he doesn't want to upset anyone, but things are getting worse in Hungary.

"We have heard," Papa says.

Mr. Kadar nods. The skin on his neck is so loose that it hangs over the collar of his shirt. He shakes his head and the skin jiggles. "There are long lines to buy even the most basic foods. Everyone is afraid of everyone else. Nobody trusts anybody anymore. Parents are afraid of their own children."

"Afraid ...?"

"Afraid of being denounced."

"What happens to those who are denounced?" Mom asks.

"The police can come at any time, even in the middle of the night. They order people to pack their personal belongings and report to the train station by afternoon. I heard from a friend that his father was taken just like that."

"With no warning?"

"None at all."

"What was he accused of?"

Mr. Kadar shrugs and his skin jiggles again. "Disloyalty to the party."

"Where are the people taken?"

"Rumor has it that they are allowed to stay in Hungary."

Mom shows Mr. Kadar the letter from her brother. He reads it over several times. "Yes, this is what must have happened to your father."

"My father is an old man. He doesn't bother anyone." Mom's voice is higher than usual.

Mr. Kadar shakes his head. "All it takes is one person to say that your father does not support the party."

Mom has her head in her hands again. I wish Mr. Kadar would stop talking about all the bad things that could have happened to Apa. What does "support the party" mean? I want to ask what party but I'm not supposed to be listening.

"When people are taken to the countryside, it's not for long, is it?" Uncle Jozsef asks. "I think what the government has in mind is just to teach a sort of lesson, wouldn't you say?"

I want Mr. Kadar to say yes, it's just for a short time. But he continues to chew for a moment. Then he stops and stares out the window. "When the people are taken to the countryside, the farmers are told to spit on them and call them names," he says finally. "If the farmers refuse, they will be added to the group to be spat upon."

I wish Mr. Kadar had never come. I wish he would get up and leave and we could eat our *palacsinta*.

"How do you know this?" Uncle Jozsef asks.

"My sister's friend got out. She is in Toronto now, and she told me."

"How did she get out?" Aunt Olga asks.

"She is old. They let old people go. In fact, they are glad if they leave. Then they take their apartments."

"My father is almost sixty-five," Mom says.

"That will certainly help," Mr. Kadar says. "Was he still working?"

"Yes."

"And what kind of work did he do?"

Mom looks down at her plate. "Before, he was a stock-broker," she whispers.

Mr. Kadar's face falls. That terrible word again. Apaguy has all these problems because he was a stockbroker. I will ask Mrs. Malone about stockbrokers and supporting a party.

"That will make it very difficult," Mr. Kadar says, looking at Mom. "I am sure my sister will do her best."

"Thank you, Mr. Kadar, sir," Mom says. "I am so very grateful." Her voice cracks.

There is a strange popping noise coming from behind me. The jumping beans are moving all around in the box.

"Look!" I shout. "They're moving."

"Let me see," Mr. Kadar says.

I take them over to his chair. "What makes them move?" I ask.

"There are worms inside the beans that are getting hot," he says.

"Real worms?"

"Of course real worms," he says.

They are slowing down, so I take them back to the light. Suddenly I wonder if they like getting hot. What if they get too hot? Will the worms die?

Gabor comes in. "Let me see," he says.

The beans are really jumping now.

"Cool," he says.

Suddenly I don't want any of them. I don't want the worms inside to die.

"You can have them," I say.

"You don't want them?"

"No."

"Thanks," he says. The word sounds funny coming from Gabor. He takes the box into my old room.

I follow him to the doorway. "Don't let them get too hot," I say, "or they'll die."

"How do you know?"

"Mr. Kadar told me," I lie.

I go back to my *paplan*. Mr. Kadar is getting ready to leave. He says what a delicious dinner it was, how he hasn't eaten a meal so good since he left Hungary. Then he says he'll do whatever he can for Apa.

"Thank you, sir," Mom says. She shakes his hand and won't let it go. "You don't know how much I appreciate your help."

"Don't count on anything," he says.

I almost say, "Hey, we forgot to eat the *palacsinta*," but I'm not hungry anymore.

When Mr. Kadar is gone, Mom really starts crying. Papa and Aunt Olga and Uncle Jozsef are all trying to get her to stop. They say that Apa is smart and strong and he'll figure something out. They say that Mr. Kadar's sister will help. Mom won't stop crying no matter what they say. I think they should leave her alone. When you're crying, you really want everybody to be quiet.

I shut the door, but I can't sleep because the skin on my back burns and itches and the letter I sent to Apaguy might get him in more trouble. I told him that Mr. Kadar would help him travel. That might make the government mad. I keep thinking about Apaguy surrounded by people who are spitting on his head and his back and his feet. The saliva is pooling in my mouth. If people were spitting at me, I would spit back. I snatched my boomerang back. I just jumped up and grabbed it.

13

On Friday, Mom and Aunt Olga make a package with matches and cocoa and two bars of the bitter chocolate that Apa loves. They put everything in a small box and cover it with brown paper.

"It's too heavy," Mom says. "I think it weighs more than a kilo."

Aunt Olga picks it up. "Between one and two, I guess." She puts the package onto the scale and puts a one-kilo weight on the other side. The package is just a tiny bit too heavy.

Mom undoes the brown paper, takes out one of the bars of chocolate, and wraps it back again. "There. Now it's okay."

They tie the package with string and write the address clearly on the outside. After that Mom sits down to write a letter to her brother. She covers two pages with her tiny handwriting. How can there be so much news when nothing has happened?

I read the beginning. She says Gabor is adjusting and I am growing and the weather is hot. She writes that Aunt Olga is going to take her driver's test soon. It is a boring letter. I fold a paper airplane out of an envelope that was in the garbage can. I want Mom to read me a book but I know she is busy now so I don't even ask.

At the end of her letter, Mom signs her real name, Maria,

and underlines it. Then she gives the letter to Aunt Olga to read.

Aunt Olga is printing capital letters on a scrap of paper.

"What are you writing?" I ask.

Aunt Olga puts her hand on mine. "Your mother is amazing. She wrote a coded letter to your Apaguy."

"A coded letter? What do you mean?"

Aunt Olga shows me. "If you take the first letter of every sentence and write it on a piece of paper, it forms a new sentence." She shows me the scrap of paper with the printed letters. "The letters spell out the message '*Oregek meg ki tudnak jonni. Surgos.*' Can you understand?"

I translate in my head. "'Old people can still get out. Hurry.' But how will Apaguy know that the letter has a secret message?"

"See the name at the end, 'Maria'? Usually your mom writes 'Marika.' That's what her father and her brother like to call her. But now she wrote 'Maria,' and see how she underlined it?"

"We decided before I left that we might need a secret way to communicate," Mom says.

"And now you do?" I ask.

Mom nods.

"Kind of a secret code."

Mom nods.

"But how can Apaguy get out from behind the Iron Curtain?"

Mom doesn't answer.

"What if Apaguy doesn't get the letter?"

Mom's arm touches my back and I wince. She doesn't notice. "I can only hope this one arrives," she says, writing *Air Mail* clearly on the envelope.

"Now can I mail my own coded letter to Apaguy?" I ask.

"No, Peti. The letter will get too heavy with so many pieces of paper," Mom says.

"But I want to send a coded letter too."

Aunt Olga says to Mom, "Let him."

I make up a secret code with squiggles and dots and dashes and zigzags. I tell him, "Hurry up and come to America. I am waiting for you." Then I include a decoder so he can read the letter. I make myself a copy of the decoder in case he writes me back in code. Right before I seal the envelope I think no, I cannot send the decoder. It might get Apaguy in trouble. I take it out and put it into the garbage can. Apaguy is a smart man. He will be able to figure out my sentence even without the decoder.

"I'll mail it for you," Aunt Olga says. "Now go out and play."

I'm not sure if she will really mail it or not. I sit on the porch. Gabor says, "Hey Peter, want a ride?"

I think maybe he's being nice, but maybe not. If I fall, my back will hurt more than ever.

"Not now."

"Come on. It'll be fun."

I walk over slowly. Gabor holds the bike so I can sit on the seat. We go around the block. Gabor is careful and steady. The wind goes through my T-shirt and cools my skin. He even helps me get off at the end. All because he burned my back, he is nice. But what about when my back heals?

14

Gabor is nicer to me but still mean to Aunt Olga. Some days he won't come out of the room for lunch. She begs him. "Gabor, you are so skinny. I fixed your favorite sandwich. Come, have some grilled cheese." Gabor doesn't answer. In the evening he says his father will never get a job because he's dumb. Gabor doesn't want to practice his violin so he fights with Uncle Jozsef about that. He lies on his back and throws socks up to the ceiling unless he's out with the boys or riding the bike. Some days he gives me rides around the block. He takes one hand off the handlebars and leans back. I don't like to ride like that.

Steven and Gabor and I go into the garage to make the helicopter spark but Steven says it's boring. He tries to make Gabor's jumping beans jump with the magnifying glass but they won't move. I think they're dead already. One of them burns. Steven puts leaves on top and soon all the beans are burned up.

"It's dangerous to play with fire," I warn.

"Is that so?" he says, adding twigs. Steven's voice is not at all like it used to be.

"It is dangerous," I repeat.

"*Papaguy,*" says Gabor.

"What's that mean?" asks Steven.

"Parakeet," says Gabor.

"*Papaguy*," says Steven. He says it with a funny accent. "I like that. I dare the *papaguy* to jump over the fire."

The fire is small but some of the flames leap up. Steven jumps over it easily. Gabor too. They know my legs are shorter. I bend my knees but I'm afraid to jump. Steven calls me a scaredy-cat *papaguy*.

Every day I wait for the mail to see if there is a letter from Apaguy, but there are no blue envelopes for a long time. Maybe Mom's coded letter didn't work. Maybe Apaguy didn't know it was a code.

I ride my bike to the library and tell Mrs. Malone about Mom's coded letter. I explain that my grandfather was taken to a farm as a punishment because he was a stockbroker. She says her great-uncle was a stockbroker too, but in New York, so he didn't have any trouble. She's very interested in everything about my family. She gives me a book to read about Communism and another one about stocks and bonds. I take them home and lie on my *paplan* and read, but they are both hard to understand and I get sleepy.

Aunt Olga passed the driver's test. She shows us her new license. In the picture, she is smiling with all her teeth showing. "Your teeth are big," I say.

Mom pulls her eyebrows together and looks at me. "Think before you speak, Peti."

It's so hot I can't sleep. The radio calls it an inversion layer. It could stay around in the Ohio River valley for a few weeks. Or it could blow out if there's a storm. I wish there were a really big storm to cool things off, but not a tornado. At school we have tornado drills and we have to crouch under tables with our arms over our heads. The siren on our school roof is so loud that when it stops, you still hear it in your ears for a long time.

I wish I had a hammock to sleep in. Then my burning back wouldn't touch the sheet in so many places. A mosquito is buzzing in my ear. I cover my ears with my hands to keep it out. When Mom and Papa come in, I fake sleep so Mom won't be mad. She always wants me to have plenty of rest.

In the middle of the night, the phone rings. It's a wrong number but I can't go back to sleep because my heart is pumping too fast. I put my hand on my chest and I can feel each time it pumps. Mom sits up.

"I thought you went back to sleep," Papa says to her. He sits up too. I can see their backs from my *paplan*. Their shoulders are touching. Mom looks small in her nightgown. Her hair is a mess all over her face.

"I'm worried," Mom says.

"Mr. Kadar will help," Papa says. His hand is on her shoulder.

Mom sighs. "It's not just Apa I'm worried about. Jozsef is not having any luck."

"Give it time," Papa says.

Mom hunches over. "I think I should get a job," she whispers.

Papa stiffens. "I don't think that is a good idea."

"You never like me to work, but it costs a lot to feed six people. The bank account is low."

Papa is quiet for a few minutes. Finally he says, "I can get a second job. At night."

"And when will you sleep?"

"But if you work, what about Peti?"

"He can stay with Olga and Gabor. Have you noticed that the boys are getting along much better now? And Olga can drive."

Papa stands up and paces back and forth in the room. He stops at the window and looks out. Then he walks some more. "Maybe you are right," he says finally.

Mom and Papa tiptoe to my *paplan* and stand over me. I keep my eyes closed but not too hard. I want them to think I'm sleeping. "He's so cute," Mom says. "Our Peti is a good boy."

"Yes, a very good boy," Papa says. He bends down to straighten my sheet. "He never complains about giving up his room."

"Peti is not a complainer," Mom says softly. "He is a thinker." Then they tiptoe around to the other side of the bed and lie down.

Soon Papa is snoring but I cannot fall asleep. I'm not sure if Mom is asleep or not. I want to tell her that I can't stay with Aunt Olga and Gabor all day, but what about the low bank account?

15

Uncle Jozsef still can't find a job, but Mom finds one right away. She has a training session at the hospital to learn how to put electric wires on children's heads to measure their brain waves.

"Why?"

"To see if maybe they have epilepsy."

"What's epilepsy?"

"It causes seizures."

"What's a seizure?"

"It's when you're unconscious and you thrash around."

"It's when you're crazy," Gabor says.

"No," Mom says sharply.

"When do you start work?" I ask.

"Monday morning at eight o'clock."

"So what time do you have to leave?"

"Seven thirty."

Mom answers all my questions. She doesn't say "We'll see" or "You are a *papaguy*" because she knows I need to know when she's leaving and when she's coming back. I check in the telephone book—the library opens at 8:00. I'll spend the day there. That's what I'll do.

Monday I wake up at 6:30 and get dressed fast. "Peti, it's early," Mom says.

"I know. I have to be at the library when it opens."

"What's the rush?" Mom asks.

"I just have to."

As soon as I get to the library, Mrs. Malone asks me if I've heard from my grandfather.

"Not yet."

"The mail service might be bad over there," she says.

That must be the problem.

"Have you read the book about Communism?" she asks.

"I can't understand it," I say.

She nods. "I'll look for something simpler."

"Do you have any more code books?"

"I think you've read them all." She tries to find other books I might like. There's one about telescopes that has neat diagrams. I trace some of them onto a piece of thin paper. Around lunchtime I ride home. Aunt Olga has made tomato soup and grilled cheese cut into triangles. At first Gabor won't come in to eat. He's with Steven and the two boys on the corner. Finally he comes in and eats two sandwiches and goes out again.

I go back to the library in the afternoon and read a book about Galileo. Nobody believed him when he told them how the Earth moved around the sun. They said he was making things up. I wonder if Galileo talked too much, like me, but none of the books say that he did. Next I read a whole book about eclipses. There's a schedule of when the eclipses will occur and where. I look at it with Mrs.

Malone, and we see that there will be one at the end of the summer that will affect North America. We look closely at the map. We should be able to watch the eclipse even in Cincinnati, although it won't be a total one. Mrs. Malone says it's important not to look directly at the sun during an eclipse. You have to look at it through a pinhole.

"How does the pinhole work?" I ask.

Mrs. Malone tries to explain it to me, but I don't really understand and the library is about to close. "Another day we'll find a book that explains it better," she says, putting her hand around my shoulders. I cringe when she touches my skin.

"What's the matter?" she asks.

"Nothing. It's just that my skin got burned."

"Sunburned?"

I could say yes, sunburned, but I want to tell Mrs. Malone the truth. "Not sunburned. Burned by the rug."

"The rug?"

"My cousin pulled me all over the apartment and burned my back on the rug."

Mrs. Malone puts her eyebrows together.

"Now he's nicer."

"That's good," she says. I like the way she never asks me to tell her more.

"I'll be here tomorrow morning," I say.

"I know," she says.

Suddenly I wonder if Mrs. Malone is tired of me. Nobody else stays at the library all day long.

"I'm counting on it," she says.

"On what?"

"On seeing you here in the morning."

"You are?"

"Of course."

When I get home, Aunt Olga says, "Peti, why do you spend all day at the library? One day we'll go to the swimming pool. How about that?"

"Okay," I say, but I don't want to go there with Gabor. He's been pretty nice these days, but when he sees that my back is healing, he might dunk me in the deep end.

16

Finally the mailman brings a blue air-mail envelope. There's no return address and the handwriting is not Apaguy's. I have Mom's work number, but she said not to call unless it's an emergency. Aunt Olga says a letter is not an emergency.

I wait for Mom at the bus stop on the corner. She smiles when she sees me holding the blue envelope. "It's not from Apaguy," I say quickly so she won't be disappointed.

"It's from my brother," she says as I give her the envelope.

"There's no return address," I say.

We walk down the street as fast as we can. Mom is holding the letter against her stomach. When we get to the door of our apartment, Mrs. Wilson is waiting.

"How long are your visitors staying?" she asks Mom.

"I'm not sure."

Mrs. Wilson hands Mom a folded piece of paper.

"What is this?" Mom asks.

"Rules and regulations. If they are not followed, you will have to move. I'm very sorry."

Mom nods. She doesn't say "Thank you, Mrs. Wilson," the way she usually does. The three of us are just standing there in front of our door. I know Mrs. Wilson wants to look inside our apartment but Mom won't open the door. I almost say "I know you want us to move," but I think about tape on my mouth.

"Well, I'd better be going," Mrs. Wilson says finally. She smiles at me but I don't smile back.

"Is there anything else?" Mom asks.

"No. Nothing." Mrs. Wilson starts slowly down the stairs. We wait. From the bottom she looks up once and then goes into her own apartment.

Mom sits down at the kitchen table with a glass of water. She drinks the whole thing before slitting the envelope carefully on the side and pulling out the letter.

My dear Marika,

I went to visit Apa on the farm, and he is doing fine. The weather is hot here too. If only this heat wave would end. We went for a swim in the Balaton yesterday. It's nice to cool off in the big lake. How is our little Petike?

My eyes move past all the other lines to the end of the letter. "His name is underlined," I say.

Mom looks quickly at the first letter of each line and puts the letters together in her head. "Apa needs help getting out," she says softly.

"What kind of help?" I ask.

Mom stares at the paper, putting the first letters together again. "Help escaping."

"Escaping from the farm?"

"From Hungary," Mom says.

"What about the Iron Curtain and the soldiers at the border?"

Mom isn't listening anymore. She calls Papa at work. "Please ask Mr. Kadar to come again," she says.

"Is he coming?" Aunt Olga asks when Mom hangs up.

"Maybe."

Quickly Aunt Olga cooks paprika potatoes with sausage and green peppers. I clean up the dining room and set the table. Then we wait for Papa and Mr. Kadar.

"Mr. Kadar said old people can leave, remember?" Aunt Olga says.

"But my father was a stockbroker," Mom says.

"Mr. Kadar's sister will find a way."

Mom keeps rereading the letter even though not everything her brother wrote is true. Like I bet they didn't go swimming. It's just a code. Maybe some of the sentences are true, but we don't know which ones. When he wrote "How is our Petike?" maybe he really wanted to know or maybe he just needed a sentence that started with that letter.

Gabor comes in to get a drink and goes back out without saying a word. Finally Papa pulls into the driveway, but Mr. Kadar is not with him. We all sit down at the table for dinner except Gabor, who won't come inside.

"I talked to Mr. Kadar," Papa says. "His sister is trying her best. She asked that we stop sending letters."

Mom stops chewing. "I just sent a package yesterday."

"We have to stop sending letters or packages."

"But last time he told us to send packages."

"I know. But now he says we shouldn't."

"Why is that?"

"People who have relatives in America are considered suspect."

"Why?" I ask. Nobody is listening to me. I want to know, but now is not the time to ask. First Mr. Kadar said being a stockbroker was bad, and now he says sending packages is bad.

Mom looks at Aunt Olga. "We shouldn't have sent the chocolate."

Aunt Olga touches Mom's arm. "We didn't know."

Papa loves the paprika potatoes and sausage. He heaps his plate with a second helping. Usually Mom is happy when he likes the dinner but today she isn't watching. She is folding her napkin into small squares.

"Mr. Kadar's sister instructed Apa to say that he has only one child, a son, in Hungary," Papa says.

"What about his daughter? Everybody knows he has a daughter in America."

Papa takes a deep breath. "He said she died."

Nobody says a word. We can hear Papa chewing and Uncle Jozsef scraping his plate with his fork. Finally Uncle Jozsef says that the dinner is excellent. My stomach is churning. I remember the jumping beans. All the worms are dead by now. The beans got burned by the magnifying glass. Apaguy has to pretend that Mom is dead. And if Mom is dead, what about me? Maybe Mr. Kadar is lying. Maybe he never even asked his sister to help Apaguy. How do we know? I don't like it when Mr. Kadar tells us to pretend Mom is dead and says that people spit on Apaguy. How does he know? He wasn't there. I don't like Mrs. Wilson either, or Steven or Gabor or Uncle Jozsef who shouts because Gabor will not practice. The only one I like is Mrs. Malone.

"Can we write to my brother?" Mom asks.

"Nobody."

Mom's face is red.

"I sent Apaguy a letter," I say.

Nobody is listening to me. I say it louder. "I sent Apaguy a letter when you weren't home."

Mom is crying. Aunt Olga says we should finish dinner, and after that we'll all feel better. She goes to the door to call Gabor again.

"There's no reason to beg Gabor to eat," I say.

"Peti, be quiet now," Papa says. "Can't you see this is not the time to talk?"

"I really did send a letter to Apaguy."

"I said stop talking."

"Gabor won't come in if you beg him," I say to Aunt Olga.

Papa smacks my hand. "Peti. Stop it."

Mom cringes. She hates it when Papa gets mad at me for talking too much. I clench my teeth and think if there were tape on my mouth, maybe I would remember not to talk. But then my skin would burn when you took the tape off. It would burn just like my back when Gabor pulled me around the house. The tape couldn't stay on my mouth forever.

17

When I go down for breakfast, Mom is getting ready to leave for work and Aunt Olga is putting sandwiches in plastic bags.

"For our picnic," she says.

"What picnic?"

"Our picnic at the swimming pool," she says.

"I can't go," I say quickly.

Aunt Olga looks disappointed. "Why not?"

"Mrs. Malone is expecting me."

"You can go to the library later, when we get back."

"But she's expecting me this morning."

Mom hurries out the door to catch the bus. I cannot go to the swimming pool with Gabor. Last night he called me a bookworm and a weirdo. What if he pulls me into the deep water? I can swim, but not in the ten-foot end.

Suddenly I think of a good reason. "There's going to be an eclipse today, so I think we'd better stay inside."

"Oh, Petike, it's going to be such a very hot day, the perfect day for a swim."

"But an eclipse can make you blind."

"Only if you look right at it. Anyway, it's not a full eclipse, right? And we'll be home long before it starts. How about that?"

Aunt Olga is trying so hard. Gabor is mean to her every

day. She tousles my hair. "Oh, Petike, you are born to worry." She smiles at me. I know I have to go.

Gabor and I are in the back of the car. The windows are down and the wind is whipping my face. Aunt Olga is driving very fast.

"My friend in Australia looked at an eclipse, and now he's blind," Gabor says.

"Completely?"

"Except for shadows."

"Except for shadows? Can he tell who his mom is?"

"Not really."

"I could tell."

"How?"

"By the smell."

"We aren't dogs, you know," Gabor says, closing his eyes.

I try not to say anything but the words burst out. "Did he look at it for a long time?"

"Huh?"

"The eclipse. Did he look at it for a long time?"

"Just for a split second."

"A split second? Did he know right away he'd gone blind?"

"How should I know?"

I shrug.

"You are a *papaguy*."

Aunt Olga looks in her rearview mirror. The car swerves.

"Stop making up stories, Gabor," she says. "Can't you see you're scaring him?"

Gabor puts his head back on the seat and sighs. I know he's wishing he were still in Australia. I'm wishing the same thing. Why can some people get visas and other people, the ones you really want to get them, can't? It just depends on where you happen to be born, I guess. Like if you're born in a country behind the Iron Curtain, it's really hard to get one. Then you have to escape across borders with soldiers. We're lucky there are no country borders near Cincinnati. We have only state borders like the Ohio River that separates Kentucky and Ohio. There are five bridges plus a ferry boat, and you don't need a visa.

Gabor is pretending to sleep. I wonder if he made up the whole story about his blind friend.

The parking lot is packed like sardines. There are no more parking spaces so Aunt Olga parks on the grass.

"We can't park here," I say. "We'll get a ticket." Maybe in Australia it's okay to park on the grass but it's not okay here.

Aunt Olga gets out of the car and opens the back door. "Come on out, boys," she says, forcing a smile. "Peti, don't drag your towel."

I wrap the towel around my arm. The grass is prickly so I run to the blacktop, but it's burning hot.

"Where are your shoes, Peti?"

"I left them at home. It's okay." I run to the entrance

gate and wait for Gabor and Aunt Olga to catch up. When Aunt Olga gets there, she shows the lady our membership card. Mom paid twenty dollars for that card so it has our last name on it, not Aunt Olga's. I want to tell Aunt Olga that we can't go swimming with that card but Gabor pulls me away.

"Pretend she's your mom," he says.

"Why?"

He pulls me all the way over to the fence. "Why can't you ever listen? Do you want to have to pay twice as much or what?"

His hand is gripping my arm too hard. I try to jerk free but he pulls harder. Why should I pretend that Aunt Olga is my mom? My mom would never take us swimming when there's an eclipse and she would never park on the grass and she would never say she was somebody's mom if she wasn't. Aunt Olga is putting the card back into her wallet.

"*Gyere*," she says. "Come on, boys. Let's go in."

Gabor lets go of me and beats me to the gate. It's the turnaround kind that I hate, with big steel fingers that can smash you if you go too slow. Gabor is in the space in front of me. He pushes too hard, and the metal finger hits my ankle. Finally I run out on the other side. Gabor is laughing.

18

Gabor and I go into the men's locker room to change into our swim trunks. Gabor gets a wire basket for our clothes, one for the two of us. I'm not sure if you're supposed to change right there or if you're supposed to go into the shower part. When I look at Gabor to find out, I see that he is wearing his trunks under his clothes, so he doesn't care where we change. I didn't think of putting on my trunks at home. I take off my shorts as fast as I can and put on my trunks. Gabor is holding a metal disk with a number on it and a pin attached to the back.

"What's that?"

"A number so we know which basket is ours. You can wear it." Gabor tries to pin the number to my trunks, but he keeps sticking my leg.

"Ouch."

"Sit still."

"I am."

"I said stop wiggling."

I tense up my leg muscles and shut my eyes. He sticks me once more. Then the number is attached but there's a drop of blood on my thigh.

After that I shut myself in the bathroom. I'll just stay in there instead of swimming. The floor is slippery with muck so I sit on the toilet seat and hold up my feet. I can see the sky above me because there's no ceiling, but I won't look up in case the eclipse comes early. I wish I were in the library so I could ask Mrs. Malone more about eclipses, like why it hurts your eyes so much to look.

Somebody knocks. "Hey, boy. You've been in there too long." I put my feet down and open the door, but I walk on my heels to keep my toes clean.

Aunt Olga is in the lap lane swimming like a swan with her head out. She has on a funny shower cap with butterflies on it, not the kind of swimming cap you're supposed to wear. She waves to me. Gabor is over in the deep area.

I find our towel and sit down. Aunt Olga swims over to the side. "Come on in, Peti," she says. "It's too hot to roast in the sun."

I sit on the edge of the pool and let the water cool my legs. Aunt Olga gets out, and water droplets from her suit drip onto my back.

"Peti, what happened to your back?" she asks.

"Nothing."

She touches my skin with her wet hands. "It looks like you have scars on your back."

I could tell her. I could tell her everything about the carpet and the money. I look at her and shrug. "I probably scratched my mosquito bites."

"Better get in the water so your skin doesn't burn," she says, splashing water onto my stomach.

I slide into the coolness of the swimming pool. The

water is crowded with kids splashing and throwing balls and jumping off the side. Nobody seems worried about the eclipse at all. I open my eyes under water. I wonder if you would get blind if you watched the eclipse from under water.

Gabor emerges right next to me. "Want to go over to the ten feet?"

"No," I say quickly, holding on to the side of the pool with both hands in case he tries to drag me there.

"It's fun over there. We can play sharks and minnows."

"I don't swim too well."

Then Gabor sees the scars all over my back. I can tell from his face that it scares him. "You want me to help you learn?"

"Okay. But right here in the three feet."

Gabor shows me how to hold my breath and float like a dead man. Then he shows me how to move my arms and turn my head to the side. He even tells me I'm learning fast. I'm glad he saw the scars to remind him to be nice to me.

The lifeguard blows the whistle. It's time to get out of the pool while he takes a break. We sit with Aunt Olga on the towel and eat our sandwiches. Gabor takes one bite but after that he won't touch it. "You know I hate salami," he says to his mother.

"I'm sorry," she says.

I wish Aunt Olga didn't feel so bad about making the wrong sandwich. I want to tell Gabor to shut up and just eat it.

"I like the sandwich," I say.

"Thank you, Peti."

Gabor rolls his eyes.

"After lunch, can we go home?" I ask.

"No, Peti. We'll swim for a while and then we'll go home."

"What time?"

"Two o'clock."

"Two o'clock? That's only an hour before the eclipse."

"An hour is plenty of time," Aunt Olga says.

There's a lady on the towel next to us who is listening. She says, "I heard about the eclipse too. I brought all these film negatives." She reaches into her beach bag. "You want some? Then we can watch the eclipse."

"I don't think so," I say quickly.

"Oh, it's fine. My husband knows all about eclipses. Right, Bill?" She taps the fat man sitting next to her. "We can watch the eclipse through these negatives, right?"

"Sure can," he says. "No problem."

But how does this man know? Mrs. Malone told me that some film is okay but some isn't, and we don't know which kind of film this is. She knows because she looks everything up in books. She doesn't just say things she heard here and there, like Mr. Kadar. Send packages, don't send packages—we don't even know anymore what's true.

My eyes are stinging from the chlorine, and the salami sandwich is churning in my stomach. I have to go to the bathroom so I head back to the building. I'll just stay there. Or I'll get a dime out of my shorts pocket and call Mom at work and ask her to come and pick me up.

Good thing Gabor pinned the disk to my trunks so I can find our basket and my shorts with the dime in the pocket. My clothes are at the bottom of the basket, under Gabor's. When I shuffle through the stuff, Gabor's shorts fall onto the floor into the muck. I pick them up fast but they are already dirty. I shake them and something falls onto the floor and rolls into the toilet stall. I open the door, and there in the muddy water is my airplane pen. Did he find it under my pillow? He must have been on my *paplan*, but when? Where was I?

I wipe my pen off and put it into my pocket. I hate Gabor even when he's being nice. I won't stay here with him. I take the dime over to the pay phone. I know Mom's telephone number. She said to call only in an emergency. But if we look up at the eclipse, we'll go blind. I hold the receiver and put the dime in.

"EEG Department. May I help you?"

"This is Peter Voros. May I speak to my mother, please?"

"She's with a patient right now. Can I take a message?"

What message can I leave? That the eclipse is coming and we're still at the pool so can she come and pick me up?

"No. No message. Thanks."

The lady hangs up. The dime falls into the belly of the phone. I drop the receiver and let it just dangle there. My arms are shaking so hard that I can't even hang it up.

After that, I wait in the locker room. I won't go back into the sun that is burning the new skin on my back. That's where Gabor finds me.

"Hey, we've been looking all over for you," Gabor says. His eyebrows are together in one line.

I don't say anything.

He grabs my shoulder. "What are you doing in here?"

"Where did you get my pen?" I ask.

Gabor lets go. "I found it on the sidewalk."

"You did not."

"You'd better thank me for finding it."

Now Gabor has both my shoulders. A man comes into the locker room, glances at us, and stands against the urinal.

I swing my legs over the bench so that Gabor can see my back. "I'm telling," I say.

"My goodness. What happened to your back?" the man asks.

"He got burned," Gabor says.

The man shakes his head. "Some burn. How'd that happen?"

"Playing with fire," Gabor says.

"A lesson well learned," the man says as he turns to go.

"We're leaving now," Gabor mumbles to me.

19

The blacktop is so hot that I think my feet will blister. I'm the first one to reach the car. There's a pink piece of paper on the windshield with little boxes along the side. The "Illegal Parking" box is marked with a check. "Violation" is written across the top in black letters. My stomach drops.

I hand Aunt Olga the paper. "They are crazy," she says, waving the paper and looking around. "What do they think? They call this grass? Do they expect me to park in the pool or what?" She looks all around the parking lot until she spots the police lady over on the other side. "Stay here, boys," she calls back as she makes her way between the rows of cars.

I cannot hear their voices, but I see Aunt Olga waving the paper and waving her arms and the police lady shaking her head. When Aunt Olga finally gets back to us, her face is bright red and my watch reads 2:20.

"Get in the car," she says, starting the motor even before the door is shut.

"What did the police lady say?" I ask.

Aunt Olga pushes the gas pedal to the floor. She doesn't answer. Gabor looks at me and pulls his finger across his lips like a zipper.

When I lean against the back of the seat, it makes me wince. My skin hurts like it did when Gabor pulled me on the rug. The rest of the way home, I make sure none of my skin touches the fabric of the seat. Aunt Olga drives so fast that I think we'll get another ticket. I want to tell her to slow down, but at first I'm afraid to talk. Then I worry that if we get another ticket, we'll never get home. Two tickets in one day and they might take us to jail.

"You're going too fast," I say.

Aunt Olga slows down a little. Gabor kicks my leg. Finally we pull into our driveway.

I get out of the car and run around the house to the honeysuckle bush in the back yard. It's dark under the bush, and the dirt is cool and damp. I stare at the black dirt. You can't go blind like that, staring at the ground. Spots of sun move on my bare legs. The metal disk with the basket number is still pinned to my swim trunks. I stole it from the pool. I have to take it back. But not now. Now is not the time.

Each sun spot has a small bite on the right side. The circles are turning into crescents. I touch one on my thigh; it gets thinner as I watch. I never saw sun spots like these before. The air is getting cooler. I shiver. The light outside is dim but there are no clouds in the sky. Just the crescents are bright, turning into thin rings of light.

The honeysuckle bush is moving. There's the edge of Mom's skirt, the black one with red rickrack. Now Mom is there with me, sitting on the dirt floor with rings of light all over her black skirt.

"It's the eclipse," I whisper.

"So beautiful."

"We can't get blind, can we?"

"Not looking at the dirt."

"Gabor's friend got blind."

"He must have looked right into the sun."

A slug moves along the ground, leaving a wet line behind. The crescents are returning. They are shiny where they fall on the slug's track. Mom pulls me to her lap. I smell her hospital smell, not the perfume-from-Apa smell that I like.

"Mom?"

"Mmm?"

"I don't want to go swimming again."

"Why not?"

"Because Mrs. Malone has been expecting me all day."

Mom has her chin in my hair and her arms around my waist. My wet trunks are getting her skirt wet.

"Mom."

"Mmm?"

"Gabor took my airplane pen."

"Did you get it back?"

"Yes."

"Your pen always comes back to you."

"The boomerang doesn't."

"But the pen does."

"And a pen is useful because I can write all kinds of codes with it."

"Apaguy will be glad you use the pen."

"But I can't write to him now." I take the pen and slant it so the airplane moves. "Someday Apaguy will come and then I won't have to write letters."

Mom doesn't answer.

"He knows you aren't really dead. He just said that," I say.

"You're right, Peti."

We watch the airplane go back and forth in the water inside the pen, and the sun spots on my legs get round again. Soon the air is hot.

"I don't want to go to the pool again," I whisper.

"You said."

"I'll stay at the library."

"Okay."

"No matter what."

"Okay."

"Mom?"

"Mmm?"

"I think my letter got Apaguy in trouble."

"No, Petike."

"Maybe."

"I wrote him many more letters than you did." Mom strokes my head. "It's okay, Petike."

"What's okay?"

"That you sent Apaguy a letter."

"Mom."

Her hands are still on my hair, smoothing down the top where it sticks up. I want to tell her about my back. I want to show her the scars that are pink again from the sun. Mom stands me up and brushes the leaves off the back of my swim trunks.

"Come now, Peti. Let's fix dinner." She takes my hand and pulls me into the sunlight.

20

Every day is hot and sticky. Papa comes home with two more fans to put in the windows. Mom bites her lip because fans are expensive. Aunt Olga doesn't say anything about going to the pool again. She gives me and Gabor nickels to buy Popsicles from the ice-cream man. Everyone is clustered around the truck—Steven and the two boys on the corner and a girl I never saw before and Gabor and me. The ice-cream truck plays "Pop Goes the Weasel" over and over. The man gives us some ice to put on our foreheads before he drives off.

"In Australia they're lucky because it's winter right now," Gabor says.

"If everything's better in Australia, why don't you go back there?" one of the boys says.

"I would if I could," Gabor says.

"Yeah. Go hang out with the kangaroos," Steven says.

The kids laugh. Gabor's face turns red. "You are a kangaroo," Gabor says.

"Takes one to know one," Steven says. Gabor's Popsicle falls to the ground. Then he turns to face Steven and pulls his fist back. I could grab his arm. I'm right next to him. Gabor punches Steven in the stomach and runs down the driveway.

All the kids chase him. I just stand there. I turn the other way. The red Popsicle is melting so fast. What if all the kids punch Gabor? What if they make a circle around him so he can't get away and then they beat him up? Steven is strong and fast. He can give Gabor a bloody nose or a black eye. I could go in and tell Aunt Olga. But she can't do anything anyway. She can't even make Gabor come in for dinner.

I walk slowly down the driveway and into the garage. I'm not hiding there. I just want some shade, that's all. A little bit of sun comes through between the cinder blocks and makes one spot on the wall. There were so many sun spots underneath the honeysuckle bushes. I wish I had a picture of the crescent spots from the eclipse. They were there for only a few minutes and then they were gone. We won't have another eclipse in North America for a long time. I might be grown up by the time there is another one. If I had a camera, then I would have pictures of the crescents on my legs and on Mom's skirt. I could take pictures of my helicopter and my airplane pen. If I lost my pen again or if somebody took it, I'd still have the pictures. I could send a picture of my pen to Apaguy. A camera is very expensive. But the book about eclipses said you can make one called a pinhole camera out of a box. That's what I'll do. I'll borrow that book again and follow the instructions.

The garage door opens and Gabor is there. His hair is sticking up. One of his eyes is swollen almost shut, and the skin around it is blue. There is a little bit of blood under his nose. He doesn't say anything. Finally I say, "You should probably get some ice."

He nods.

Gabor is leaning against the cinder blocks. I should help him walk up the driveway. I should get ice out of the ice tray and put it into a dishtowel for his eye. He put ice on my burns. But first he pulled me around the house by my feet.

"Don't use my icicle," I say.

"I won't," he whispers.

We are staring at each other. Gabor limps up the driveway.

When I go inside, Gabor is in my room practicing the violin. It must be hard to play the violin with your face all swollen. I wonder if he put ice on his eye. I wonder if Aunt Olga saw it. She is in the kitchen cutting carrots. I open the freezer to get ice cubes for my water, and the big icicle is still there.

"Did you get a Popsicle from the ice-cream man?" Aunt Olga asks.

I nod.

"What about Gabor?"

"He got one too," I say.

She smiles at me. "We are having lasagna for dinner," she says.

I take the cup of ice water to my *paplan* and pick up a book I borrowed about black holes and theories about how the Earth started. It's hard to read but I like it anyway because it has pictures of the Earth from far away. I wonder how they took the pictures, from farther even than an airplane flies. On the cover of the book is a picture of all the planets and the sun. It's a drawing, not a photograph, so you don't know if it's true or not. I like photographs better. When I grow up, I'll be a photographer. I'll carry my camera everywhere.

The doorbell rings. I get up and open the door a crack. There is Mrs. Wilson. "Is your mother home?" she asks.

"No."

She tries to poke her head in but I won't open the door any wider.

"Please tell your parents that your guests will have to leave by the end of the month."

I don't say anything.

"Did you hear me?"

I nod.

"Can you remember that?"

I don't answer. Mrs. Wilson is waiting, but I won't say yes. Our guests are not bothering her. The notes of Gabor's violin are coming out into the hallway. For a minute I think Mrs. Wilson is listening to the song. It is lively and fast, like a dance. Then she shuffles down the hall.

21

I wake up early, but Papa is already gone. I have chocolate milk with Mom.

"What are you doing today, Peti?" she asks.

"Going to the library."

Mom looks at the weather report in the paper. "It's going to be very hot, Peti. Are you sure you don't want to go for a swim?"

"No." My voice comes out too loud.

"You know, they have swimming lessons at the pool next week. Maybe we will sign you up. I could drop you off on my way to work."

"I don't want swimming lessons."

Mom finishes her coffee. "Okay, Peti." She pats my head. Then in a low voice she says, "What's the matter with Gabor? He hardly comes out of his room."

I could tell her. Mom is rinsing her cup in the sink. She has to get to work on time. "I don't know," I say quickly.

When I get to the library, I look on the shelf for the eclipse book, but someone else has borrowed it. Mrs. Malone checks the cards in the catalog and says there are other books about pinhole cameras, but she will have to request them from a bigger library. They will be delivered on a truck in a couple of days.

"How many days?"

"I'm not sure. Two or three."

I wish I could get the books right away but there's nothing to do about that. I look out the window. There are big gray clouds in the sky, and the wind is making the branches move. Mrs. Malone says it looks to her like a cold front coming. We find a book about weather patterns in southern Ohio, and it says that cold fronts come from the west. We go outside to check, and sure enough, the wind is blowing from west to east. "It's probably already storming at my brother's in Indiana," she says.

It's funny how I never think of Mrs. Malone as having brothers and sisters and parents and children. I never think of her anywhere except in the library. "Where do you live?" I ask her.

"In Kentucky," she says, "just across the bridge."

"We're lucky you don't need a visa to come across the river," I say.

She nods. "But for some people, that used to be a very hard border to cross."

"It was?"

"Before the Civil War, the river was the dividing line between slave states and free states," she explains.

I learned a little bit about the Civil War in school last year, but I want to hear more.

"Escaped slaves tried to get across the river in tiny wooden boats and rafts. Some even tried to walk across the ice in winter or swim across in summer," Mrs. Malone says.

I cannot even swim the length of the swimming pool. I

would never have made it across a river. "Did some people drown?"

"I'm sure they did. The river water is cold and full of whirlpools."

"Did children swim across too?"

"I'm not sure."

Mrs. Malone gets me a book about slavery. It has a picture on the cover of a man with very dark skin picking cotton in a big field. It's some kind of print but not a photograph. The first chapter talks about something called the Underground Railroad. It's not really a railroad at all, just like the Iron Curtain's not really a curtain. It's a way for slaves to escape from the South to the North by hiding in people's cellars and walking at night. I wish Apaguy could escape like that, but there are too many soldiers at the border.

Mrs. Malone gives me some thin paper, and I trace the escape routes. I don't notice the time going by until she says, "You'd better get home before the storm hits, Peter."

The wind pushes my bike sideways. I have to stand up to pedal even on the downhill. I wonder what the slaves did once they came across the river. The book says Cincinnati was a very important station on the Underground Railroad because Ohio was a free state and Kentucky wasn't. Still, when the escaped slaves got to Cincinnati, they could be caught and returned to their masters. That doesn't seem fair, after everything they had to do to get across the river.

When I get home, Aunt Olga says she's worried about me riding in this wind but I tell her I'm fine. She opens the kitchen window to let the cool air in. "How about staying home this afternoon?" she says.

I don't want to, but the rain has started. Aunt Olga has to close the window because the wind is blowing water all over the kitchen counter. Gabor comes in soaking wet and goes up to his room without saying anything. Aunt Olga sighs. She doesn't even call him for lunch because she knows he won't come. Sometimes I think she likes me better than she likes her own son.

We eat ham sandwiches together. I tell her that I'm going to make a pinhole camera but I have to wait for the books to come in, so now I'm reading about slavery. She says that happened a long time ago.

"It's not that long ago," I say, "compared to when the Earth started."

Aunt Olga is putting away the milk. "Peter, you are reading too many sad books," she says. She looks really worried. "When I was your age, I just read funny books."

"I don't like funny books," I say. "I don't like comics either. I like real books with real pictures."

"You are a serious boy," Aunt Olga says, patting my hair.

A clap of thunder shakes our apartment. Aunt Olga pulls me to her lap. "I'm not scared of storms," I tell her, looking out the window.

"When Gabor was little, he was so scared of thunder," she says, covering my ears with her hands. I try to imagine Gabor as a six-year-old but I can't. "You know, he really was a sweet boy," she says, smoothing my hair back from my forehead.

"That was a long time ago," I say. Sometimes a short time can seem long and a long time can seem short. It all depends on what you're doing.

Rain is pounding the sidewalk in front of the house and making rivers on the edge of the street. I want to fold a paper boat and float it down the street but Aunt Olga is worried that I'll get struck by lightning.

By the time Mom comes home, the rain has let up and steam is rising from the street. Gabor slips out the door. I sit on the sofa and read a chapter about a slave family trying to get to Canada. They came across the Ohio River at night and hid in the cellar of a freed slave's house. The next day, they had to hide in two coffins and pretend to be dead. A carriage was supposedly taking the coffins to a cemetery, but instead it drove them to the next station on the Underground Railroad. I wonder what the escaped slaves were thinking when they were inside those dark coffins with no food or water or light. Maybe a little light got in through a crack. I hope so.

Uncle Jozsef bursts into the living room. "I got a job," he says.

"What is it?" Aunt Olga asks.

"I'm selling encyclopedias."

Aunt Olga doesn't say anything at first. "Who will buy them?" she asks finally.

"I can tell you that tomorrow after I sell them." Uncle

Jozsef says that he'll have a certain territory, and he has to go from one house to the next and explain the encyclopedia pamphlet. He has one in his pocket. It has a picture of the set with gold edges on the pages. The information inside each volume is new. I'm sure people would like to buy this kind of encyclopedia.

"How much is it?" Aunt Olga asks.

"You have to pay only three dollars a month. That's all."

"For how long?"

Uncle Jozsef looks at his information. "I'm not sure."

Aunt Olga goes into the kitchen. Mom follows her. I know they're whispering about this new job. I stay with Uncle Jozsef and ask him about the encyclopedias.

"Does it tell you about the planets?"

"Of course. It has a whole section under *S* for 'solar system.'"

"What about slavery?"

"That's under *S* too."

"What about codes?"

"Oh, yes. It has all kinds of codes."

"I want to learn the Morse code," I say.

It turns out Uncle Jozsef knows the whole Morse code alphabet. He writes it down for me with dots and dashes, and then I practice writing secret messages. The first thing I write is *Congratulations*. Uncle Jozsef can read it even without a decoder. He picks me up and spins me around.

At dinner, Aunt Olga doesn't say a word. I know she

wanted Uncle Jozsef to be an accountant, so I say, "There is a lot of accounting when you sell encyclopedias."

Gabor zips his lips at me. I look away. After dinner I draw circles with bigger and bigger bites out of them on a piece of paper so I can remember the eclipse. I still wish I had had a camera. Maybe the books will arrive at the library tomorrow. Mrs. Malone said two or three days but it could be just one.

Gabor is outside with the boys on the corner. They are laughing and talking. They don't seem like they want to beat him up anymore. How can they punch Gabor one minute and laugh with him the next? I guess things are like that. You can send packages one day and you can't the next. You can be a slave one day and free the next. Or you could get caught. Papa escaped from Hungary in the middle of the night. A guide showed him the way across fields and streams. If he'd been caught, he would have been killed. Then I would never have been born. You never know how things will go.

At the top of my picture, I write *Eclipse, August 14, 1952*. That way, when I grow up, I will be able to remember when the sun and the moon and the Earth lined up and the shadow of the moon took bites out of the sun. Even fifty years from now, I'll remember.

22

There is shouting coming from my old room. I glance at the clock. The hands are lit up in neon green. Eleven thirty.

"How can it be lost?" Aunt Olga shouts.

"I know we put it there," Uncle Jozsef says. "I have to buy my first set of encyclopedias."

"You have to buy them? I thought you had to sell them."

"I have to buy the first set."

Uncle Jozsef and Aunt Olga are shuffling things around and throwing things against the wall. They are looking for the money. I wonder where Gabor is. I look out the window. Bugs are flying around the streetlamp. It's very late. He cannot be outside.

I lie back down on my *paplan*. The boomerang is still there under my pillow, and the helicopter and the airplane pen too. I hold the pen and tilt it. I know the plane is moving, but I can't see it in the dark. Even when you can't see things, sometimes you know they're happening. Like I know that I am not alone in the room.

I stand up quickly and turn on the light. For a minute I cannot see, it is so bright. Then my eyes adjust. There are the old photos of Mom and Apaguy and me on the night-stand with the neon-green clock. I open the closet door. Hiding behind Mom's dresses is Gabor.

"Tell your father what happened to the money," I whisper.

"You took it," Gabor says.

"You told me to."

"You still took it."

We hear a crash from my old room. Gabor's face is all twisted. If I had a camera I would take a picture of it like that. Twisted and scared.

Mom's silk dress, the one she wore when Mr. Kadar came, slides off a hanger onto the floor. "Pick it up," I say.

Gabor stares at me.

"Pick it up," I say again. "It's my mother's favorite dress."

Gabor reaches down and the door of the room opens. Mom is standing in the doorway.

"What is going on?" Her voice is hoarse. "Do you boys know what happened to the money?"

Gabor is holding the dress in front of his face. Mom's eyes meet mine.

"Remember the red bicycle? The new one Steven was riding?" My voice cracks.

Mom puts her hands to her forehead. She smoothes her hair back. "Peti, we have enough to worry about without—"

I cut her off. "I know."

"Peti, why—"

I turn toward my mother and shout so loud that Mrs. Wilson can probably hear me in her apartment. "So do I."

"You do what?"

"I have enough to worry about too."

Mom's voice is deep and calm. "Peti, you have nothing at all to worry about. You have food to eat, a roof over your head. You even have a bicycle."

Mom's face is blurry in front of me. "I never even got to ride the new bicycle," I say, staring at Gabor.

Tears are running down his face. You can still see the purple bruise and the scrape under his eye from where Steven punched him. Then they are all there, Uncle Jozsef and Aunt Olga and Papa.

Slowly I unbutton my pajama shirt and start to pull my arm out of the sleeve. My back has healed but the scars are still there. I'll show them what Gabor did. I'll show them.

"I'll pay back the money," Gabor whispers. He throws the dress onto the bed and runs out of the room. I put my arm back into the sleeve of my pajamas.

I cannot fall asleep. The fan in the window is making a clicking sound. Mom and Papa are still not in bed. Then I hear Aunt Olga crying and Papa's deep voice. "Everything will be okay," he tells his sister.

"What about Gabor?"

I cover my head with my pillow so I can't hear what Papa says. I don't care if Gabor comes back or if he doesn't or what happens to him. I'm going to make a camera and be a photographer. I'll go up in a rocket and take pictures of the planets. I'll take pictures of Earth and Neptune and Mars. There are no borders between planets. Just air. Not even air. Nothing.

23

Aunt Olga takes Gabor to register for school. I put a piece of bread into the toaster and push the button down. The coils turn red hot. The bread pops up and I spread it thickly with butter and jam. Mom says I have nothing to worry about. I have everything I need. I have bread, butter, jam, and a toaster. I have a *paplan* to sleep on and a helicopter and an airplane pen and a fake boomerang. But that is not all that I need. I need a camera that can take real pictures. And I need an apartment without Gabor.

I pick up the pamphlet about the encyclopedias. *Super scientific, up to date*, it says in gold letters. How will Uncle Jozsef pay for the encyclopedias without the thirty dollars? And if he doesn't pay for them, he'll lose his job. Then they'll have to stay in our apartment forever.

The mailman is early. He brings us four advertisements but no blue envelopes. Mom will look at the mail as soon as she comes into the apartment. She always looks at the mail before she even says hello. If there's no blue envelope, her mouth will be in the thin line and there will be nothing I can do.

I finish my toast and pour a bowl of cereal. If I had a camera, I would take a picture of the funny reflection of my face in the shiny toaster. I'll go to the library and see if maybe my book is waiting.

I pass my old room on the way to the bathroom. Everything is still all over the place. Nobody bothered to pick it up. The suitcase is open on the floor. I took the money out of the pocket on top. Gabor told me to get the money but he didn't make me. Nobody made me. Nobody can make you do things you don't want to do. But Uncle Jozsef makes Gabor play the violin. Somebody made Apaguy leave his apartment and go to the farm. Somebody made the slaves pick cotton. Brave people say no. Brave people try to escape. Maybe Apaguy is not like that. He could be afraid like me. I'm afraid of deep water and mean kids. But then brave people can get killed too.

Outside the sky is clear and blue. The storm really did cool things off. I take my bicycle out of the hallway. I am about to head to the library when Mrs. Wilson stops me.

"Peter, did you give your parents the message?"

I don't answer.

"Cat got your tongue?"

I shake my head.

"No, it didn't, or no, you didn't tell your parents?"

"I didn't tell them yet."

She lifts her eyebrows.

"They have a lot to worry about right now," I say.

"Speak up, Peter. I can hardly hear you. Say what you mean, loud and clear."

"We have a lot to worry about right now," I say, louder. "So I didn't tell them yet."

"I don't have anything against your guests, really. It's

just a rule of the apartment. That's all." Mrs. Wilson smiles. I've never seen her smile before. "Do you understand?"

"Yes," I say. "I understand."

I take off down the street on my bicycle.

"You're late today," Mrs. Malone says when she sees me.

"Are my books here yet?"

She shakes her head. "They should arrive tomorrow or the next day." She looks at the calendar. There is a red X in tomorrow's square.

"Why is there a red X?" I ask. After the words are out of my mouth I know I'm being too nosy. It is Mrs. Malone's calendar, not mine.

She smiles. "That's my day off."

"What if my books come?'

"There will be another librarian here."

"Another librarian. Who?"

"I don't know. Maybe Mrs. Lipton."

I can hardly imagine someone else sitting in that chair behind that desk. "Mrs. Lipton might not know anything about pinhole cameras."

"I don't know much about them either, Peter. It's all in the books."

Suddenly I wonder if Mrs. Malone is sick of kids like me. Maybe she just wants to read her own books. "What do you do when you take a day off?" I ask.

"Sometimes I clean my house or visit my brother."

"The one in Indiana?"

"Yes. That one. Or I take a day trip somewhere."

"Where do you go on a day trip?" I'm asking too many questions but I want to know.

"Well, tomorrow I'm going to see the Rankin House."

"The Rankin House? What's that?"

"It was a station on the Underground Railroad."

"A real one?"

"Yes. Now it's been made into a museum, so I want to go and see it."

"Can I go with you?" The words come out without my thinking about them first. Papa always tells me to think before I speak. Mom too. I shouldn't ask Mrs. Malone to take me someplace. Maybe she wants to take her own nephew or somebody. Maybe she likes to go places by herself.

"I was just going to suggest that," she says. "Ask your mother and we'll make it an end-of-summer field trip."

"What if my books come in and I'm not here to get them?"

"They will wait for you," she says.

We spend the rest of the day looking at maps of the Underground Railroad stations. There are a lot of them near the Ohio River. The book says sometimes slaves made quilts as a secret way to show the route to freedom.

"Kind of like a secret code," I say.

Mrs. Malone nods. "That reminds me. Have you heard from your grandfather lately?"

I shake my head. "He's not allowed to write to us anymore."

"That's too bad." She looks really sad. "Can you write to him?"

"No. Not now." I trace some of the lines on the map with my finger. Kentucky, Ohio, Michigan, and across the border into Canada. "Escaped slaves weren't really safe even after they crossed the Ohio River," I say.

"That's right. Some people captured escaped slaves and took them back across the river into Kentucky."

"Why did they do that?"

"Money. They got a bounty for each returned slave. You know, money is the motivation for lots of things."

Mrs. Malone is looking at the map. She is planning our day trip to the Rankin House. She doesn't see that my face is all red. Money. Thirty dollars. One twenty and one ten, from the pocket of the suitcase. Before we go, I have to tell her. I open my mouth, but the words will not come out.

Mrs. Malone is writing down the directions. When she's done, she folds the paper and puts it into her purse. "You know, Peter, I wonder if I would have helped slaves escape."

Mrs. Malone has a soft face with curls around it. And she is nice. She helps me find secret-code books. But she doesn't seem so brave. I'm not the brave kind of person either. I would never try to swim across the Ohio River or walk on ice. I'm afraid of loud voices and baseballs that come too fast and rug burns. Maybe I would have helped a slave escape. Maybe not.

"I don't know," I say.

24

Gabor has been put back a grade. Since he came from Australia, the principal said he should repeat the sixth grade. They think schools in Australia are behind schools in America, and that makes Gabor mad. He is slamming doors and splashing water all over the bathroom.

When Uncle Jozsef comes home, I ask him if he sold any encyclopedias.

"Not yet, Peti. It will take some practice."

"We'd better polish your shoes," I say. "They're all scuffed up."

Uncle Jozsef isn't listening. Something is breaking in my old room. "Stop it," Uncle Jozsef shouts, flinging open the bedroom door.

"I'm going back to Australia," Gabor shouts.

"You are going to work to earn the money you stole," Uncle Jozsef shouts back.

"Please." Aunt Olga is begging them to stop.

Gabor is holding up his violin. He is about to throw it, but Uncle Jozsef grabs it first.

I don't want to watch them anymore. I don't want to hear Uncle Jozsef's loud voice and the sound of things breaking. I'm tired of all that. I go outside and walk slowly down the street. The boys on the corner are not out. Neither is Steven. I walk around the block. A few people are standing at the window of the Dairy Queen. I have a dime in my pocket. Enough to get an ice-cream cone. I stand in line. If I had a camera, I'd take a picture of the boy sitting on the bench with ice cream all over his chin. Then I'd take a picture of the chain-link fence with vines growing up it.

"What'll it be?" the lady asks me.

"One dip of vanilla with sprinkles, please."

She pushes the button and the ice cream comes out in a thick coil. She adds the sprinkles and hands me the cone. I sit on the bench near the little boy and eat my ice cream. People come and go. A man and a lady walk up to the window. They are both wearing red shirts and they are both laughing. They buy one ice-cream cone and take turns licking it. I wonder if they had only enough money for one cone or if they like sharing it. They smile at me. I'd take a picture of them too.

When I get home, everyone is quiet. Aunt Olga and Mom are putting dishes away. Uncle Jozsef is reading the paper. I spread newspaper on the linoleum so I can polish Uncle Jozsef's shoes.

"Mrs. Malone wants to take me someplace tomorrow," I say to Mom.

"Where?"

"To a place where they used to help slaves escape."

"Who is this librarian?" she asks. "We don't even know her."

"I know her," I say. "She's nice." I am swirling the polish in circles.

"Peti, you cannot go with a stranger."

"She is not a stranger," I say. My voice is getting louder. "I see Mrs. Malone every single day except on her days off."

Mom looks over at Papa. He is watching the news on television, something about soldiers in Korea. She looks back at me. "Where did you say this librarian wants to take you?" Mom asks.

"A station on the Underground Railroad." I could explain about the slaves and the secret codes, but the television is blaring.

"Boys like trains," Aunt Olga says. "Let him go."

"Okay, Peti," Mom says.

25

I toss and turn on my *paplan*. It will be strange to be with Mrs. Malone outside the library. It will be strange to sit in a car with her instead of at the small round library tables. I feel for the airplane pen underneath my pillow, but it's not there. My stomach flips. Did Gabor take it again? Or Steven? I feel in the pocket of my shorts. There it is, just where I put it. I turn on my light and read another story about the slaves. In every story, the slaves escape to freedom. That's the name of the book—*Escape to Freedom*. They don't write books about the slaves who didn't make it.

I hear Mom's footsteps on the stairs, but I don't pretend to be asleep. "Peti, it's late."

"I can't sleep."

Mom looks at the book in my hand. "If you stopped reading, you could fall asleep."

"But I want to read," I say, moving my eyes quickly across the page. Finally the family made it across the border and they could come out of the coffins. I bet it took a long time for their eyes to get used to the light.

Mrs. Malone is wearing shorts and a straw hat. She doesn't look the way she usually does, in her dress and lipstick. She hands me a picnic basket. "For later," she says. "When we get hungry."

"I'm always hungry," I say.

"Then it's a good thing I brought the picnic."

"What did you pack?" I shouldn't ask that. But I want to know.

"Peanut butter and jelly sandwiches. And a surprise."

"Peanut butter and jelly?" I am sounding like a *papaguy* again. I want to know what the surprise is but I don't ask.

We sit in the car. "We're going to take the scenic route," Mrs. Malone says. "It may take a little longer, but we aren't in any hurry, are we?"

"A little," I say.

"Why is that?"

"My library books might come."

Mrs. Malone nods. "I see."

It takes a little while to get out into the country. We drive along the river. The houses are small. Some are falling apart. A little girl is helping her mother hang clothes on the line. Their house is boarded up across the windows.

"I wish I had already made my camera," I say.

"I brought an old one."

"You did?"

"My father used to take lots of pictures, and when I was helping him clean out his closet, I found this camera."

"Was there film in it?"

"As a matter of fact, there was."

"There was? Did you have it developed?"

"I did."

"What were the pictures of?"

Mrs. Malone is driving carefully around the bends in the road. "Some were of me and my brother when we were little kids."

"How old were you?"

"I was maybe seven and he was eight. We were fishing in a stream behind our house."

"Did you catch any fish?"

"In the picture, my brother is holding a fishing line with a fish on the end. He is smiling."

"What about you?"

"I wasn't smiling. I remember I hated it when the fish was thrashing around with the hook in its mouth."

"Why did you go fishing if you didn't like it?"

"I liked to go with my brother. I just didn't like actually catching the fish."

I nod. It's funny how a camera clicks for a second so you don't know what happened before it or after it or the next day or a little farther down the stream. "That film stayed in the camera for a long time," I say.

"More than thirty-five years," Mrs. Malone says. "I'll bring that old picture to the library and show it to you."

While Mrs. Malone drives, I inspect the camera. It's one of those that you look down into from the top. I look through the car window at everything going by. The road veers away from the river and goes up a small hill. There is a farmhouse near the top with a dilapidated barn next to it. A man is plowing the field on a tractor. If the camera were mine, I'd take a picture of that.

We stop at a rest area and have the sandwiches and some fruit she brought. The surprise is cookies in the shapes of stars and moons. I make my shadow cover the edge of the moon cookie. "I'm making an eclipse," I say.

The Rankin House is way up on a hill above the river. It's big and white and it has a porch. A lady at the door gives us a pamphlet saying that more than two thousand slaves were hidden there from 1825 to 1865. The slaves would come across the river in boats or on rafts. They knew which house was safe because there was a candle burning in the window all night long, kind of like a secret message. The Rankin family had thirteen children, and they all helped to keep the slaves hidden in their house and barn during the day. Then at night the slaves went on to the next station on the Underground Railroad.

In the back room of the house there is a small museum with lots of old pictures. There is a photo of the Rankin family. The mother and father are in back, with very serious faces, and the children are in front. The older ones are holding the little ones on their laps. I wonder if they liked helping the slaves. I wonder if they were scared. You can't tell from the picture.

There is also a picture of a man with scars all over his back from being whipped. I have to look away or I'll throw up.

We go out on the porch and look down at the river. With

the sun shining on the water, it looks so peaceful. You can't see the whirlpools or tell that the water is cold. Bees are buzzing around the black-eyed Susans by the steps that go all the way to the water.

"Do you want to walk down to the river?" I ask Mrs. Malone.

"How about I watch you from here," she says. "I'm too old for all those steps."

I'm not sure if I want to go alone. But Mrs. Malone has already settled into one of the rocking chairs on the porch. I really want to see the water up close. I walk through the tall grass and to the top of the steps.

"Peter," Mrs. Malone calls.

I turn toward her voice.

"Here. Take this." She is holding the camera out for me. I can't believe she will actually let me take her father's camera. She hangs it around my neck. "Use up the film," she says.

It's on number six out of twenty-four. Eighteen pictures. I can hardly believe it.

The steps are narrow and steep. When I get halfway down, I take my first picture, of a bee on a Queen Anne's lace. Then I take one of the steps from the bottom, the way it must have looked to the slaves once they got off the rafts.

The riverbank is full of black rocks like coal. I look across at the Kentucky side through the camera lens and take a picture of that. The river looks much wider from here than it does from the house. How could anyone swim that far?

I look up at the Rankin House. The slaves couldn't see the house at night but they could spot the candles in the windows. Then they knew which way to go. But any house could have had candles. What if they went to the wrong one?

I take more pictures of the house, the rocks, a log, a fishing boat. I wonder how long it will take to get the film developed. Maybe one week. Or ten days. It can't take longer than that.

26

I fall asleep in the car on the way back. When I open my eyes, we are in front of my house.

"Thank you," I mumble, trying to wake up.

"You're welcome, Peter. See you tomorrow."

I think I should say something more. "Thank you for the cookies."

"You're welcome again."

Nobody is home. I open the mailbox and there is a single light blue envelope. I can't tell if it is from Apaguy or not. There is no return address. The postmark is smudged. The handwriting doesn't really look like Apaguy's. I hold the envelope up to the sunlight, but I can't read anything through the paper.

Mom and Papa are at work. Uncle Jozsef is selling encyclopedias. I don't know where Gabor and Aunt Olga are. My stomach feels unsettled from all the winding roads. I pour myself a glass of water and get some ice cubes out of the freezer. Where is my icicle? I bet Gabor took it. He set it in the sun and let it melt. I was saving that icicle. I found it on the roof gutter in December. Now it is August. For eight months I kept it in the freezer and now it is gone.

The door opens. Gabor and Aunt Olga are there. "Where's my icicle?" I ask Gabor.

"What icicle?" Gabor asks.

"The one I was saving."

"How should I know?" Gabor heads down the hall.

"Oh, Peti. I didn't know you needed it. I was cleaning the freezer." Aunt Olga is patting my head. "And it was just taking up space."

"What did you do with it?"

"Why, I put it in the sink."

"And it melted?"

"Of course it melted."

I know it doesn't make any difference. I can find another icicle next winter. But it might be thinner or shorter. Mom knew the icicle was mine. She left it alone. I wish Aunt Olga wouldn't always rearrange things.

I try to drink my ice water, but I swallow wrong and water spills out of my mouth and onto the blue envelope. I pick it up quickly but the ink is already running. Aunt Olga sets it on a towel to dry. The towel gets a blue stain.

"Don't worry, Petike," Aunt Olga says. "Soon we will be leaving."

"Leaving?"

"We were just out looking for an apartment."

"An apartment?"

"You didn't think we would take your room forever, did you?"

"I like the *paplan*," I say.

"I know. But you've had enough of us."

I should say, "No, it is fine. You can stay with us as long

as you want." That would be the polite thing to say. But the words are stuck in my throat. Gabor is my cousin. That's what Mom told me on the way to the airport. He plays the violin. He is Aunt Olga's son. I pick up the soggy envelope and stare at the smudged letters. "Did you find an apartment?" I ask finally.

"Not yet."

"Aunt Olga?"

"What is it?"

"It doesn't matter about the icicle."

"Okay, Peti."

"I'll miss seeing you every day."

"You are a good boy, Peti."

Gabor goes out the door. He doesn't say "Bye" or "I'll see you later" or anything.

"Come back soon," Aunt Olga calls after him. "It's almost dinnertime."

Gabor doesn't turn around.

"You shouldn't beg him to eat," I say.

"You are right, Peti," Aunt Olga says.

I watch Gabor cross the street. I don't care where he is going or when he is coming back or if I ever see him again.

Aunt Olga empties a bag of green beans into a bowl and runs water over them. Together we snap off the ends. "Did you have a good time at the railroad station?" she asks.

I could tell her that it's not really a railroad, it's just a name like the Iron Curtain, but it seems like too much to explain. "It was fun," I say.

Mom does not open the letter right away. First she wants to have a cup of coffee.

"Why don't you open it?" I ask.

"I will. Give me a minute."

Mom doesn't ask about my trip with Mrs. Malone. She forgot all about it. She asks Aunt Olga about the apartments. One was too dark with only tiny windows. One was so close to the train track that you could feel the floor shake when the train went by.

"I would like to watch the trains," I say. No one is listening. I say it again, louder.

Mom shuts her eyes and sighs. I know she is thinking that I won't stop once I get something in my head. Finally she swallows the last bit of coffee and slits the blue envelope. She takes out the thin paper and unfolds it on the table. The corner is wet but the rest is okay. I read over her shoulder.

Dear Maria,

The fall weather here is beautiful, and the farmer and I have become good friends. He has taught me a lot about raising chickens and pigs and corn. Now I am strong and healthy from fresh food and sunshine.

My eyes skip to the end of the letter. *Love, Apa*, it says, and the *Apa* is underlined.

"It's a coded letter," I say.

Mama is still reading.

"The letter is made up," I say, pointing to the underlined signature.

Aunt Olga's eyes follow my finger. "Peti is right," she says.

She writes down the first letter of each sentence. I look at what she has written. *"Nem kezdhetem ujra az életet Amerikában,"* it says. "I cannot start a new life in America." That's all. Not "I hope I can get out soon." Not "Please help me escape." Not "Someday I'll come and see my Peti."

"So he's not coming," I say.

Mom keeps looking at Aunt Olga's printed letters.

"I am glad he finally wrote," Aunt Olga says. "At least we know that he is doing okay."

"How do you know?" I ask.

"That's what he writes," she says.

"But it's not true. It's just for the code," I say.

"Some of it might be true," Aunt Olga says. "Anyway, at least it's a letter."

"He's not coming," I repeat.

"Not now," Aunt Olga says.

"Never," I say.

Aunt Olga puts her hand on Mom's. Mom is crying without making any noise. Her tears are making the ink run even more. It's a big mess.

"We can call Mr. Kadar," Aunt Olga says.

Mom shakes her head.

"The librarian had a camera," I say, "and I took some pictures."

Aunt Olga raises her eyebrows. "Of what?"

"The Ohio River, the Rankin House, a log. Lots of stuff." Mom is blowing her nose. "After we get them developed, I'll send some to Apaguy," I say.

"That would be nice," Aunt Olga says.

"We can't send anything," Mom whispers. Her voice is hoarse.

"I know. But when we can, I'll send them," I say, putting my hand on her arm.

The doorbell rings and Aunt Olga goes to open the door. "Yes, Mrs. Wilson," she says. "We will be gone by the end of the month."

27

Two of the library books are not yet in, but one of them came. It has a long history of the pinhole camera, how it was discovered in China in the fifth century BC and then by Aristotle around the fourth century BC. Now people just use pinhole cameras for fun. It gives basic instructions for making a simple one out of an oatmeal box. The thing is you need photographic paper. Where am I going to get that? In the book there's a picture of a homemade pinhole camera. It's big and clumsy.

Mrs. Malone is busy today. Work piled up while we were at the Rankin House. I won't ask her about the pictures I took on her father's camera and when she can get the film developed. I won't ask her about the fishing picture from when she was little. She has work to do. I'll think about tape on my mouth.

I browse through the books on the shelves, pick out a mystery, and start reading it, but my mind wanders. I look up *camera* in the encyclopedia. It shows how the lens works, how it takes the light and splits it. But how can light split? I look up *eclipse*. There is a picture of the crescent of light but only one. I saw so many under the honeysuckle bush. That's because the honeysuckle leaves were like lots of pinholes.

My stomach is growling. Maybe I'll go home early. Mrs. Malone sees me by the door.

"Sorry I'm so busy today," she says.

"What about the pictures?"

I forgot about the tape on my mouth. Mrs. Malone smiles. "I meant to tell you. My father has a darkroom in the basement, and he said he would develop the pictures with you."

"A real darkroom?"

"Yes, a real one."

"When can we go?"

"We'll see."

I don't like it when people say "We'll see." Sometimes that means they'll forget about it. But Mrs. Malone is not like that. She said we would go on a field trip and we did.

"I'll call him tonight and we'll set a date."

"Okay."

"Oh, and here's the old picture I was telling you about." She takes a photo out of her wallet. A boy with a big smile is holding a big fish. I can't tell if the fish is still alive or not. The girl has her eyebrows together and her arms crossed.

"You were mad," I say.

"I wanted my brother to throw the fish back into the stream."

"Did he?"

"I don't remember."

I look at the picture for a long time. There's sunlight on the stream, and rocks in it. It's narrow and shallow.

"Where was your father standing when he took the picture?"

"I don't know, Peter. When we go, you can ask him."

My stomach growls so loud Mrs. Malone can hear it. "You'd better eat a good lunch," she says. "And I'd better get this pile of work done."

"Can I borrow that old camera?" I ask. I didn't plan to ask that, but now it's too late to take the words back.

"We can ask my father."

"I want to take pictures to send to my grandfather."

"I see."

"I want to show him that I still have the pen and the helicopter." Suddenly I have an idea. "Maybe you could take a picture of me with the pen in one hand and the helicopter in the other."

"I thought you couldn't send him letters now."

"I'll get the pictures ready and put them in an envelope with the stamps and the address and everything. That way it will be ready."

"That sounds like a good idea," Mrs. Malone says. She sighs at the pile of papers on the desk. I know she would rather talk to me than do all that paperwork.

My bicycle tires are crunching small acorns on the sidewalk. It's not fall yet, but they are already all over the ground. When I get home, Aunt Olga is cleaning up the kitchen.

"I signed a lease," she says.

"A lease? For an apartment?"

She nods.

"When are you moving?"

"September first."

I count the days in my head. "That's in less than two weeks."

"Yes, Peti."

"Does this apartment have big windows?"

"A few."

"And no train?"

"No train."

"Where is it?"

"On the west side of town."

"We are on the east side."

"I know. But the west side is cheaper."

"What if Uncle Jozsef doesn't sell enough encyclopedias? Then will you move back with us?"

"I don't know, Peter."

"How did Uncle Jozsef buy the encyclopedias without the thirty dollars?"

"He borrowed money from your father."

"From Papa?"

"Yes, from Papa. And now Gabor has to work to pay it back."

"I took the money out of the suitcase."

"I know. But Gabor is much older. He should know better."

"I know better too."

Aunt Olga is scrubbing the countertop. "I'm sorry that Gabor has not been nice to you," she says.

I don't know what to say. I'm sorry too. Maybe he'll be nicer someday. I don't really care.

"All this moving around from country to country has been hard on him," she says.

In my mind I see Gabor crossing one border after another. But he crossed from Australia to America on an airplane and we were waiting for him at the airport. He didn't have to look for a candle in the window or swim across a freezing cold river. There was nothing for him to worry about.

"You know, in Australia we moved eleven times."

I haven't heard much about that before.

"Why?"

"Looking for jobs. At least Gabor could carry his violin everywhere we went."

"I think he hates it."

Aunt Olga stops scrubbing. "It is the only thing he has," she says.

After lunch I go upstairs to my *paplan* and wait for Mom to come home. I wind the propeller of the helicopter, but no sparks come out. I think it is broken. The boomerang too. It never came back, not even once. But the little airplane in the pen still works. I tilt it back and forth and watch the plane move from one end of the pen to the other.

Tomorrow Mrs. Malone will tell me when we're going to her father's to develop the pictures. Maybe we'll try to make a pinhole camera too. It might be good for taking pictures of things like eclipses but not for people eating ice-cream cones. Maybe I can borrow her father's camera for that. We'll just have to see what kind of camera is good for what.

The doorbell rings. There is Mrs. Wilson. "They're moving on September first," I say before she has a chance to ask me anything.

"Actually, I came to see if your cousin would like to sweep out the garage. He said he was looking to earn some money."

"I'll ask him."

I go to the door of my old room. I could just walk in. It's still my room. But I knock.

"Who is it?"

"Peter."

Gabor opens the door a crack. He is putting his things into the suitcase.

"Mrs. Wilson wants to know if you want to sweep the garage," I tell him.

He doesn't say anything.

"I can help if you want."

He tosses his socks into the suitcase, and his shirts, and his shorts. Then he shuts the suitcase, sets the violin on top, and heads out the door.

Gabor reaches the cobwebs on the ceiling. I hose out the garbage cans. He sweeps the floor. I pick up the piles. We don't say a single word. When we are done, Mrs. Wilson looks around the garage and gives Gabor a five-dollar bill. "For the two of you," she says.

"Thank you," I say. Gabor doesn't say anything. He puts the money in his pocket. Mrs. Wilson says she'll have more work for us tomorrow. She goes into the basement.

"Only twenty-five more to go," I say to Gabor.

He doesn't look at me. He is standing so the light hits his foot. If I had a camera, I'd take a picture of him like that, squinting into the sun.

"Tomorrow," he says.

"Tomorrow what?"

His eyes meet mine. "Tomorrow we'll earn five more." Then Gabor heads up the driveway.

I stay in the garage for a few minutes. It looks different all cleaned up. Mrs. Wilson said she may ask us to paint the walls next week. I shut the door and it is completely dark except for a crack in the cinder blocks. That would be easy to fix. Maybe I can make the garage into a darkroom. Then I can develop my own pictures. I can make them big or small, however I want. Tomorrow Mrs. Malone will let me know when we are going to her father's to develop the film.

When I open the garage door, the sunlight is so bright that I can hardly see. I bet my pupils are as small as a pinhole. Smaller, even. Then my eyes adjust and I walk slowly up the driveway after my cousin.